Found Documents from
the Life of Nell Johnson Doerr

FOUND
DOCUMENTS
FROM THE LIFE OF
Nell Johnson Doerr

A Novel

Thomas Fox Averill

University of New Mexico Press ～ Albuquerque

Library of Congress Cataloging-in-Publication Data
Names: Averill, Thomas Fox, 1949– author.
Title: Found Documents from the Life of Nell Johnson Doerr: A Novel /
    Thomas Fox Averill.
Description: First edition. | Albuquerque: University of New Mexico Press, 2018. |
Identifiers: LCCN 2017036424 (print) | LCCN 2017040294 (ebook) |
    ISBN 9780826359315 (E-book) | ISBN 9780826359308 (softcover:
    acid–free paper)
Classification: LCC PS3551.V375 (ebook) | LCC PS3551.V375 F68 2018 (print) |
    DDC 813/.54—dc23
LC record available at https://lccn.loc.gov/2017036424

Cover photo: *Gypsum Hills Tornado*, by Lane Pearlman, licensed under CC by 2.0
Designed by Felicia Cedillos
Composed in Adobe Caslon Pro 10.25/14.25

This book is dedicated to my second family,
the Goudies.

PREFACE

This volume is inspired by a single moment one summer when I was between appointments at the University of Kansas, in Lawrence. I walked into the Natural History Museum to see the restored diorama built by that intrepid adventurer, Lewis Lindsay Dyche. No trip to Dyche Hall is complete before a quick descent to the basement, to see the fossils of Kansas. I was rewarded with an entire exhibit, running throughout the summer and designed to inspire children: to help them to understand, and even to look for, the fossil past. *Fossil Discoveries in Early Kansas* was not a large exhibit, and many of the fossils were fragments, but that is what we can still discover today.

I made a discovery for myself. Where possible, the discoverer of the fossil was credited, and the name Nell Johnson Doerr was ubiquitous. Who was this Nell? How did she become interested in fossils? Where might I find more about her? With my phone I took pictures of each of her finds, with names and dates of discovery, most from the late 1860s through the 1880s. Her birth and death dates were not listed, but the fossils she had discovered told us much about our ancient past, and I set about discovering her.

Serendipity entered when I made a trip to the Watkins Community Museum, home of the Douglas County Historical Society. Looking for references to Nell Johnson Doerr in their collection of reference volumes and files, I found that, indeed, an early Lawrence resident was named Doerr. I searched records for an address, then walked immediately to the stone house where Nell had lived. The current resident allowed me access to an old barn behind the house, and in the rafters, on a small shelf, I found a valise, leather and fading to dust, and I knew—with the same certainty Nell Doerr must have had in discovering her fossils—that I had found what I was looking for. The contents of that valise have provided all the material for this small volume, which I hope honors the memory of an amazing nineteenth-century woman. I have edited her letters and notes and diaries and have selected from many documents, and from her many drawings, to shape this account. I have not transcribed everything, as the entries are often standard, as when they note weather and temperature. She might embellish some of these, as in: "Temperatures above normal, meaning suffering rather than hot, and again I curse the widow's weeds that carpet me on any excursion from home." Or, about the cold: "February has so seeped into the house that the flaming fireplace is an image of warmth, but not warmth itself." Or, the simple: "Rained all day, so no venturing. Read until eyes tired."

In spite of these less than scintillating entries, repeated as they are on occasion, Nell Johnson Doerr has in her diaries moments of great disclosure, worried wrestlings with the direction of her life, finely detailed accounts of her relationships with people, with ideas, and with herself.

Due to the sensitive nature of certain materials, I have changed some names to protect those people and their heirs. Other historical figures, like Hugh Cameron, the Kansas Hermit, and Benjamin Mudge, of early Kansas geological fame, are too well-known to be disguised.

In this account I hope to reveal what I consider to be the most important stories of Nell Johnson Doerr's life, restoring an important woman to the historical record. If I have failed, the valise and its contents have found a home at the museum and can be seen by anyone. Others might find in the many documents a different story than the one I have selected and shaped.

YOUR HUMBLE EDITOR

Letter from Solomon Doerr

My dearest Nell—

I hope that all is well with you in Pine Bluff. I write with news of a successful journey. The road from Pine Bluff to Fort Smith, I must note, is populated with soldiers, traders, Indians, preachers, sinners, and all manner of thieves. I kept my cargo well-hidden, though at great discomfort to them, lying as they were under the wagon boards as though occupying their coffins. The bales of tobacco above them I shared with passersby quite freely, for men ask fewer questions when so well met.

Still, I worried that I might later be attacked when I crossed into Indian Territory, so I made certain to display my rifle and pistol even as I was most jocular with whomever I met. Only at night, once we made it onto the road that went north to Fort Scott, could I allow my true cargo some air, an air untainted by the slave holders of Arkansas and Missouri. For two days, however, I was joined on the road by a detachment of United States Cavalry dispatched to investigate an outlaw band said to be based in Springfield and terrorizing the countryside, stealing cattle, mostly. We rode together comfortably enough. I masqueraded as Samuel Dorfman, tobacco trader, eager to make my shipment to Fort Scott and points north.

They did not suspect my contraband cargo, nor my destination— Lawrence, Kansas Territory, newly founded by the Massachusetts Emigrant Aid Society, as we have read in the newspapers. And a fledgling town I find here, Nell. Thinly populated, but with a righteous people. I was immediately able to put these former slaves in good hands and wish them Godspeed north to Leavenworth, where I found my contact, then on they go to Canada and freedom. They were a brave father and mother, with one knee-high son, quietly suffering the necessary demands of their journey. Only little Carolina sickened, and I fear she might not live to enjoy the freedom she deserves. Surely if these souls can make such sacrifices then we, too, are right in our plan to join them in Lawrence. They are abolitionists, yes, but they are here to develop a city, a state, and to prosper as many of them already have prospered in their Massachusetts homes. I like their business sense, and I have already laid claim to several fine pieces of property south of the Kansas River, and have invested in lots along the platted streets of the town. The city will grow quickly to the south, sprawling beneath and climbing up a hill they have already given the elegant name Mount Oread.

I will be staying here for at least another fortnight, securing our interests, before I am able to return to you in Pine Bluff. You must proceed with any preparations that will help us to sell our interests there, and begin making plans for what we need to move, and what we need to leave behind. Do not overstrain yourself. I know you are a hearty woman, but in your condition you must think of another besides yourself. I am eager for what awaits us, Nell.

Your loving husband,
Solomon

Unsent Letter

Thursday/Saturday, September 20/22, 1854
Pine Bluff, AR

My Dearest Solomon:

I received your letter of September 10, and though I contemplate leaving my home and family with some trepidation, I hear in your words your conviction and anticipation for this move and what it will bring to us and our cause. I will proceed as you suggest, though Hiram, kind brother that he is, has already offered a generous amount for your land and house. He will rent it to a man newly arrived in Arkansas, a man named Smith who is a smithy by trade—you will appreciate the economy of that coincidence, no doubt. I will speak to this Smith about his interest in those of our possessions either unneeded or too unwieldy to move to K.T.

I shall be the largest article, no doubt, for I am swollen near to bursting with this baby. I can only pray that my bulk means a strong, healthy baby. In spite of Mother Jo's reassurance, I am still haunted by the miscarriage of baby Benjamin, and your absence, though necessary, means I do not have your strong hand to hold, nor your hearty words to buoy my spirits when I wonder at how fickle life can be. Others carry their children with ease, without my seeming fear, trusting themselves as animals do. I envy them. Mother Jo lost her first baby, then Mary and Hiram came healthy and strong from her womb. She and her experience comfort me.

I will finish this letter in the morning, for I tire in the late afternoon, and sleep through evenings like our old dog, dreaming of rabbits, no doubt, as I will dream of you, my dear husband.

Late afternoon, Saturday

All that I wrote has cursed me. Horrible nights, terror-filled days. Pain and fear in equal measures. I cannot bear to send you news, dear Solomon. That which was to sustain us, to make us into a family, has again disappeared, slipped away, been kicked from our path like a wayward stone, sunk into the underbrush, forever hidden and useless. Just as I am utterly useless. You will return to . . . what? Emptiness? Grief? Disappointment? To a woman dispirited beyond reason. I cannot send you this letter. I cannot. I cannot break such news by post. I am breaking, broken.

Diary Entry

Saturday, October 28, 1854
Lawrence, K.T.

In leaving my Pine Bluff home, I feel compelled to write in this small book. What was once the easy unburdening of myself—to Mary, or to Mother Jo, or to Hiram's Penelope—now must find a different form. Though I am far from home, I do not wish to be far from myself and my thoughts.

Solomon and I were invited to attend the Thanksgiving dinner provided by Levi and Louise Gates, northwest of Lawrence. I did not want to attend, still mourning the loss of the boy child who was not to be. In that time separate from Solomon, having lost the child, I could not manage. I did not dress myself for two weeks. I did not speak. I could hardly take nourishment beyond broth and tea. I awaited Solomon's return from K.T., and the telling.

He was full of Lawrence. He was struck down by the news of our loss, but his heart kept room for the bright prospects of a new home. He spoke of it with more enthusiasm than he had in his letters, in part to rally me from my grief. Against the wishes of our parents, we did name the child together—Lawrence—and we shed our tears over the small mound, dug next to the grave of our dear Benjamin, who had also withered in my womb. Such small graves, but harder to dig for their size. Father Robert and Hiram said they never felt a heavier burden. So it was for Solomon, too, grief upon grief, terrible for its repetition. 1850, 1854, and I, perhaps childless evermore. Solomon, in spite of the loss, remained definite. We would leave for Lawrence in one week. He declared his love, though I did not doubt it, reassuring me that we, even if it were only the two of us, were a family, and sufficient unto ourselves, bound together, and bound toward a future as any family might be. The touch of his hand, my head on his shoulder, his handkerchief for my sudden tears, his knowledge that I might survive my feelings and thoughts—all these made me love him the more, even as he spoke his love for me.

And so I was spirited away, leaving all my spirit behind. Yet we were determined to use our lives to make a difference, and K.T. gives us that opportunity. Slowly I have regained composure and wit, though I know many in our new home think me odd, or shy, or reclusive. Solomon said so when prodding me toward accepting the generous dinner invitation. Gates is an important man in the town, Solomon told me, and likely Charles Robinson, of real stature here, would attend. I agreed to go, and a fine meal it was. Much was said of the future of Lawrence. Much was said about the ruffians who had ordered the Gates from their land that very morning. Only the offer of the doughnuts that were to be our dessert prevented them from violence, their stomachs more important than their principles, I suppose, and so we were thankful to have no dessert. Louise is a fine woman of fine spirit, content to live on the edge of civilization, thankful for her log home, just completed.

We ate out of doors, a prairie chicken pie thanks to Levi's skill in shooting. The prairie chicken is perhaps more savory to the eye, flushed and thrumming from the grasses, than it is succulent to the palate. The beef was provided by cowboys on the California Trail willing to sell a lame steer. Winter squash and beans and cornbread filled the table. Robinson, Reverend Lum and his lady, and young men writing for Eastern newspapers filled the seats. I had not felt the gratitude the day called for, but as I ate and heard others give thanks and predictions of the importance of where we are and what we are doing here, a glimmer of pride in Solomon, and even a pride in myself, rose in me enough that I was able to join the toast to the future. We toasted, of course, with water. People here are spirited, but do not condone spirits. Slowly I am regaining myself. Dare I move toward hope? Dare we move beyond words, Solomon and I? What a place we find here, as raw to the view as I am in my heart. I am a settler here. And I will settle myself, as well.

Letter to Mother Jo

Dear Mother Jo:

Even when I am with Solomon, or in the barely constructed home of friends, or between church and quarry, or on our main street, Massachusetts, I feel alone. The Kansas sky is huge. Lawrence has no trees but for the gangly cottonwoods, willows, and sycamores that drink at the river. A sea of grass to walk across, to build upon. Build we do, arduously now, as though our activity were antidote to our isolation.

Wagons are filled with coarsely milled lumber, with rock, with nails and hinges. They creak and groan, men shout at their oxen and mules and each other, all as coarse as their lumber. We try to build a town, Lawrence, Kansas Territory, and yet each day as houses are framed, as stone is laid upon stone, we seem, in this vast landscape, to shrink rather than grow.

Because of the scarcity of wood, Solomon has chosen to build our home of rock. An abundance of what they call "limestone" lies beneath the surface of the hills and makes up the bluffs above the Kansas River. Small quarries have been in operation since the first settlers from Massachusetts arrived. We haul the largest, flattest stones, as many as we can each day, to our lot. Solomon seems to know what he is doing. "Like the barn foundation Father and I built in Arkansas," he says, "only we'll stack it to eight feet before we lay on roof joists and raise the rafters."

Mother, how will the Kansas walls know to stand, when rocks, stacked, always lean in Arkansas, and fence lines crumble, pushed and prodded by water, or by tree roots? Solomon tells me not to worry. "We're building to last. I've paid extra for the best mortar."

I want to believe him. I do believe him, as honest and fine a man as he is. I don't doubt him, but perhaps more myself. How will I stand? Yet I will. I should not use the word "roots" in Kansas, but I can say we will build upon the foundation of rock. We must have a solid future here, together, as we accomplish the rudimentary necessities of home building and then turn to our truer mission of building a Kansas free of slavery. First, we are slaves to rock and work, to isolation, even desolation, to grass stretching to the horizon, to a sky that portends weather in its own dramatic way. Sometimes I shudder to live under it.

This is to say that I miss you, Mother Jo, and Father Robert, and Hiram and his Penelope, and their Josephine and Antoinette, and I miss Mary and her Michael, and their Sara and John. I say their names, with prayer, comfort, and longing in each syllable. Please write, for each word from you and from Mary shrinks distance, sets loneliness at bay, helps to set my path more firmly toward what I know I must endure.

Your loving daughter, Nell

Diary Entry

*When Solomon planned to build the foundation of our house just as his father had
built the foundation of their barn in Arkansas—deep, with an extra wall, to create a space in which human flesh might be secreted, I told him such an accommo-
dation should not be necessary in a Kansas Territory we mean to make free.
"Here, of all places, will we need to hide those slaves we are bringing to freedom?
Surrounded as we are by fellow abolitionists? No," I insisted, "we will not."*

*"Perhaps you are right," Solomon agreed. "But if not for slaves, for shelter." He
pointed out the design of the Unitarian Church, soon to be constructed on Ohio
Street. "A large room built into the rising earth—shelter and safety, for our cargo
and ourselves, just as for the church." If we might need it, he pointed out, we
might as well build it, and though I long for openness, and though I moved to
Lawrence that we might help slaves without so much danger as in slave-ridden
Arkansas, and though nothing might begin the elevation of that race so much as
being seen—as people, as fellow travelers, as tablemates at dinner, as equals
though once downtrodden, and seen publicly as that, in deed as well in word—I
dropped my argument. Solomon, I knew, would most likely insist on his plans,
and he is so often correct, and my continued objections would only create obstacles
in what should be a clear path. And so we built as he planned, and a fine house
we have erected around us.*

*Just last night a woman, Bessa, and her children, Samuel and Joshua, were
brought to our home, as scheduled, to take supper with us, spend the night, then be
transported by Solomon to Leavenworth. Bessa was a thin, light-skinned
woman, and her children were each a darker shade—one toast and one burned
toast. Their eyes were red with lack of sleep, with worry, and though they were*

obviously exhausted they did not settle easily at the table. Frightened, I finally realized. They were still frightened, even though they were among people who of all on this earth most believed in their freedom. Still, they rushed through their supper, nearly perched on their chairs, and when we set pallets on the floor, they looked to the windows. Solomon, sensing their fear, whispered to Bessa. She nodded her head. He pointed to me. "They will feel safer in the basement below," he said. "Will you lead them down?"

They slept in that damp room Solomon had insisted on constructing, safe, though likely uncomfortable. Through the floorboards I heard the boys, twice, cry out, then sob. Bessa hushed them, humming in a low voice a mournful tune that haunted me. They must be haunted themselves, I thought, trying to rest, to sleep again, still terrified by the accumulation of days of slavery, whether ordered about, whipped, abused by each other or a master, ripped from husband and father, ripped from bed, ripped from normal human life by the degeneration of slavery.

They were here, in our home, and we would rise in the morning, and they would clean their faces, and we would feed them a hearty breakfast and slake their thirst and load them boldly into our wagon and hie for freedom. Surely their spirits would be lifted by their proximity to freedom. Surely they would settle into a peace that would transcend their fear. I wanted them to know Emerson, his "He who is not every day conquering some fear has not learned the secret of life." Surely their bodies would find comfort rather than pain, the lines in their faces smoothing just as their lives would smooth. Freedom would impress upon Bessa a new tune to replace mourning.

Bessa, Samuel, and Joshua arose and climbed the ladder into our kitchen. Their countenances still spoke of fear, in spite of my wishes for them. How they longed for safety and freedom. How I wanted to wipe care from their brows over breakfast. I thought to reassure, so I spoke a single word into the silence. "Soon," I said.

Bessa's eyes widened and filled with tears. She shook her head. "Soon," she repeated, though more as a question than with eager hope.

"Soon be free," I said, repeating that line from the Negro song.

"No soon about it," Bessa said. "You all helping us, thank the Lord, but we got miles and time ahead of us." I nodded my head in sympathy. "Samuel and Joshua wish to be back in Tennessee, where they could eat regular, sleep in beds, play with the others. They understand food and beds and foot races and church services better than the miseries of freedom."

"Miseries?" I asked her.

"We was slaves, back in Tennessee. But we was more free than since we run."

"Are you sorry you left?" I asked, taken aback.

"No," Bessa admitted. She patted her hand as though comforting herself. "What lies ahead is most important. But it ain't soon."

"Yes," I said, for in some way she was speaking for me, too, for my own experiences since leaving Arkansas. The trouble of being in K.T., the suffering, the miseries I'd brought upon myself, miseries shared in freedom with Solomon, but miseries nonetheless. "I came here, too, from a place more comfortable, and I am not sorry either."

So we left it. We finished our breakfast. Bessa helped me to clear away the dishes and put the chairs against the wall, and Solomon brought his wagon, and loaded Bessa and her boys, and they left me. I have made a full day of thinking upon Bessa while cleaning, washing clothes, taking a light supper, and hoping for Solomon's speed—perhaps a return late tomorrow evening. I see her loaded into the wagon. I see Solomon hoisting her boys next to her. I remember the two boys we might have had, Solomon hoisting them into a wagon for a journey. And then I see nothing. At least Solomon will return to me. God willing. It is God's will for all of us, and not our own will, though we will people toward freedom.

Letter to Sister Mary

Wednesday, June 20, 1855
Lawrence, K.T.

Dearest Mary—

The mud here is terrible. My clothes will not come clean. My shoes have holes, and all leather goes to the repair of saddles and harness, as tack and animals are more important than humans. The dry goods has only three colors of muslin, and so I and my fellow citizens walk the streets in obvious patches, looking like French harlequins but with no humor. Fuel is in scarce supply, and Solomon and I pay dearly for what we then hardly dare use. I underestimate what I must burn for a gristled roast and potatoes and use those precious twigs, branches, and logs only to eat raw meat and underdone potatoes. So, too, with oil. If I read in the day because I am starved for light at night, I am deemed lazy for not working sun up to sun down as do all the others. If I read at night, I waste oil, precious and dear, that should be used only when guests arrive, or for the sacred reading of the Bible, or for enough light to wash and change into my bed clothes. I sleep on a mattress of straw ticking more likely to be full of vermin than to be a rich invitation to full rest.

"Civilization will come," says Solomon. "Nothing great was done but through suffering."

Mary, I have left Arkansas, and family, and the two babes earthed in our family plot. I have given up my cows and pigs and chickens, my garden, my precious roses nodding with dew in dawn light. I have given up trees altogether, and make do with grass. I have given up streams and creeks for ditches and draws. I have given up shade for punishing sun and gentle rain for cloudbursts. I have given up rushing rivers for slushing, silting drainages a half mile wide and eight inches deep. Before we dug our well, water here had to sit for a time, that the dirt might sink to the bottom of the bucket. I fear I have given up my heart, along with everything else.

And yet my heart is here, too, with my Solomon and our work to carry slaves to freedom, our mission to make Kansas Territory the Free State of Kansas. Duty calls each moment, yet duty is synonymous with a suffering I find it hard sometimes to bear. Yet bear I must. You have always known me to be long-suffering, and a dutiful wife, and a woman dedicated to my decisions. Solomon tries for reassurance, and most often succeeds. His hand in mine, his grip, his smile, his pleasant words—they are Arkansas to me, compared to the harshness of Kansas. I try to remember to laugh when Solomon is light in his mood, so that we might encourage each other.

Thank you for hearing me out. I write to you, Dear Mary, rather than Mother Jo, though I know your intimacy, how you share each detail. Perhaps you will share, but only after reflection, for I write without decision, and perhaps only to see my concerns on paper and thereby know myself to be the fool I am in my self-pity.

Your loving sister, Nell

Letter to Sister Mary

June 8, 1856
Lawrence, K.T.

Dearest Mary—

I write to you with equal parts anger and grief. What was said to number eight hundred blackguards from Missouri followed Sheriff Samuel Jones into Lawrence on May 21 and sacked the town. They entered the newspaper offices first, of course, the printing presses destroyed, and the type sunk to the bottom of the Kansas River because of the "seditious" words that could be made with their letters. This reaction to Lawrence comes from men who probably do not know their letters, and when they do, they utter such obscenities as Stringfellow's diatribes in his *Squatter Sovereign*; like all Southerners, he labels Lawrence a "Northern invasion," writing that "though our rivers should be covered with the blood of their victims and the carcasses of the abolitionists should be so numerous in the territory as to breed disease and sickness, we will not be deterred from our purpose." After this attempt to eliminate free speech, they razed the Free State Hotel and set it ablaze, claiming it was built as a fortress. Those who saw it done report that the ruffians were only slightly above animals in their demeanor. They walked on two legs, though some staggering from drink. Their hair and beards are long and stringy, their bodies stinking for lack of cleanliness, their teeth black as pitch. "Devils," said Olivia Johnson, who promptly hid from them in her basement and was not molested. It is no wonder they seek to make everyone their enemies, for they have few friends. To seek mastery, they abuse their slaves; to seek reputation, they denigrate the reputations of those around them.

The spread of slavery is their purpose. And ours? To stop the spread of slavery. Yes, slavery is legal in the United States, and by extension it is legal in Kansas territory. But our intention is to soon vote for a Kansas constitution that will prohibit the institution from setting its pernicious roots here. We assemble at the hotel. We print our arguments in the Free State Press. Assembly and free speech are our rights as citizens. Should we not have as much right to promote our positions as they have to defend theirs, no matter how vile each thinks the other to be?

They do not believe so. They invaded the home of Charles Robinson, then proceeded to burn it to the ground. Mr. Samuelson says they carried a blood-red flag with the words "Southern Rights" sewn into the fabric. Yes, nothing but blood and destruction—of human beings, of freedom, of property—follows the banner of the Southerner.

None were killed, for most of us citizens deserted Lawrence as quickly as it was occupied by these foul-mouthed revelers in violence. They finally left us, and we put out fires and settled into our homes once more. Mary, we are unsettled, but out of this destruction, and out of our grief, we will rise again, rebuild, and print our arguments for freedom.

Captain John Brown has struck back with violence. He and his sons, and some of the band they call the Pottawatomie Rifles, all a stern group of men, took their revenge by murdering five Pro-slavery men not far from Lawrence. Captain Brown was already infuriated, as were we all, by the caning of Senator Sumner in what should be sanctified chambers. Brown considers himself an arm of a vengeful God, and his wrath will ever terrorize the Pro-slavery heart when he nears. Brown has succeeded in terror, though so has Sheriff Jones, so all of us fear more terror, more revenge, more destruction, more violence.

I grieve this loss of civility, peace, and hope. All lips speak of war, and our Kansas soil will no doubt soak up yet more spilled blood. For now, we are safe. For now, we rebuild. For now, we continue to nurture K.T. as a Free State, soon to join the Union.

Pray for us, Mary. We are equal parts hope and fear. As such, we have come to understand even better the plight of the slave, who, without freedom, lives at the whim of a cruel, selfish master. Such is the South, as you know from our years of work, the work Solomon and I are determined to continue.

You have expressed your eagerness to visit us in K.T. Please do not risk travel in this direction. Arkansas is barely safe. Indian Territory is not safe. Southern Kansas is not safe. The Kansas-Missouri border is dangerous, with loaded guns on both sides facing each other. When we have our Free State constitution, when this matter is settled, I will welcome you to our humble, but free, home.

Your loving sister, Nell

Letter to Mother Jo

Saturday, July 10, 1858
Lawrence, K.T.

Dear Mother Jo—

I hope all is well with you and the family in Pine Bluff. Should you come visit me now, as you have promised during these years of our separation, you will find improvement. Solomon paid dearly for lumber enough to build the front porch he has for years promised me. A grand porch it is. Instead of the rudely stacked stone stairs we have climbed to enter our door, wide wooden steps rise to a porch floor eight feet deep and spanning the entire front of the house. Columns hold a slanted roof so that we can sit in shade, protected from all the elements that might have kept us indoors. Solomon has built a railing, with spindles, and matched their form with a lattice that hangs from the porch eaves. All is painted white so that it gleams in the morning sun. We are as decorated as any home in Pine Bluff, and I sit on the porch greeting those who pass by, feeling as though I am a queen dressed in brocade and lace, though it is but my porch that is so dressed.

Many join me to sit for a time in comfort and tell me of their husbands and children, of the books they read, of news from families back East. Winnie Terrant lost a mother to the grimmest of symptoms as conveyed in a well-worn letter. Sadie Gilbert shared details of a niece's wedding held in Boston. Olivia Johnson pulled a lock of her dead sister's hair from an envelope and drenched her handkerchief with tears over such a fine, gentle, kind soul lost to a fall from a horse. Others have porches, of course, but all feel they must come for at least one visit on the new Doerr porch.

Nearly four years here in K.T. now, Mother Jo. We have planted trees—oak and walnut—and lilacs, and roses. We have hedges sprouting between homes, grapes growing along wooden fences, vegetable gardens dug between small saplings of apple, cherry, peach, and pear. The fruit will come. This week I will dig potatoes, unearthing meal after meal from what is good soil. The new potatoes, so crisp and bright last spring, eaten with peas, showed the promise of a rich harvest. I will not be disappointed.

Solomon remains ever busy. I could not have found a more temperate, honest, hardworking, gentle man for the sharing of my life. His journeys with our precious cargo, delivered most often to Leavenworth, have put him in business with a variety of growers and manufacturers. He has kept Lawrence in various supplies of garden tools, plows, axe blades and hammer heads. He has found inexpensive bedding and blankets. Once, he secured trunks of women's dresses, more than enough for those of us starved for manufactured clothing, a rarity but not an impossibility at Solomon's price. With the profits from these business endeavors he is able to purchase land at the edge of our growing town, lots and farms that will appreciate in value as Lawrence thrives. In just four years, Mother Jo, our population has grown to nearly two thousand souls.

I hope you will contemplate a visit, though I know it is hard for you to leave all of your duties at home and in Pine Bluff. Your letters are my touchstones, and I eagerly await your next. Love to Father Robert, to Hiram, Penelope, Josephine, Antoinette and the new Joyanne—you must pinch her cheek for me—and to Mary and Michael, Sara and John. How I miss all of you. Yet know that I am well taken care of, too.

Your loving daughter—
Nell

Diary Entry

The Planter's Hotel, Leavenworth. These walls house me and Solomon. And the Honorable Abraham Lincoln, who wants to be president. He spoke at Stockton Hall for over two hours, his second speech in this city, by special request, as so many clamored for him to repeat for others what he had so logically and eloquently outlined last Saturday evening.

Solomon, in Leavenworth on business, and hearing Mr. Lincoln's first address, bid me haste, and I flew to secure a carriage and make the journey with Mr. and Mrs. Browder, who were also eager to hear the man said to have bested Senator Douglas in debate and thereby garnered the attention of the nation.

Abraham Lincoln is raggedly imposing, a rail of a man, all knuckles and knobs, chin and ears, dressed in clothing shambled by his travels. His hair is not so disheveled as that of Mr. James Lane, as Lincoln cuts it closer to his head. Still, when this orator trains his eyes upon an audience, this group of citizens completely filling Stockton Hall, and including women, and opens his mouth to put forth his arguments in clear and simple language, he suddenly seems an elegant figure. Though his voice is high-pitched, even shrill, as ungainly as his body, his discourse soon smooths his voice from awkwardness to surety.

Others, more certain of the facts, or interpreting them differently, might criticize Lincoln's speech. Not I. I have lived through the consequences of the failure of our government's policy that he so vigorously condemns. Those framers of our Constitution may have tolerated, and the Constitution itself does tolerate, the institution of slavery, but none of these men ever endorsed it, and they consistently made laws to inhibit its spread. They knew, as we have known for years, of its injustice. The policy of squatter sovereignty, as a part of the

Kansas-Nebraska Act, ignored this fact and allowed for the spread of an immoral institution, and it ignited partisan violence in Kansas Territory. The nation is fighting over K.T. and fighting over the extension of slavery. Yes, we believe, first and foremost, that slavery should never be extended. We wish, too, for the abolition of slavery, but, as Captain Brown proved, we still have a government that will not brook violence and insurrection.

John Brown, hanged but days ago, was a great man, a divine man, a prophet. He will be a martyr to all who oppose slavery. Lincoln does not approve of him, his murdering bloodshed and treason. Lincoln is a man of the law. As such, he is criticizing a law that allows the extension of slavery. In Kansas we have triumphed. The Wyandotte Constitution, so recently passed by a rightfully elected and judicious delegation, including my own Solomon Doerr, has put Kansas in a favorable position, poised as we are to become a Free State in what we hope will soon be a country free of slavery.

This nation has executed a great man, treasonous and addled as John Brown became in his righteousness. On this day I have seen another great man. He rises from conflict as so many men and women have risen in Kansas Territory. He will be one of those who helps to decide the future of the United States, because he knows so well our past.

When he finished his speech, I stood. Others rose around me, equally transfixed by his argument. After all, we have lived with the violent consequences of squatter sovereignty, with that terrible opportunity for slavery to spread. We did not want to leave the hall, as we were so well understood in our struggle, and in that warm flush of well-spoken words we were nurtured in our hope for days to come. These were fine antidotes to the bone-cold weather we would all face on our journeys home.

Solomon, how propitious your business in Leavenworth, that it coincided with the visit of Abraham Lincoln. How timely your message to me to come to you. How much in partnership are our minds and hearts. The war for Kansas is over. I retire to my hotel bed well-pleased, eager for the future we have both so fervently hoped for.

Sketch of Solomon Doerr.

Diary Entry

Hooves thundered into Lawrence, careless riders careful to kill men and boys—not women, the thieving gallants—and then throw torches to homes. Solomon insisted I hide, and he pushed me to shelter under the floor of our home, wrapped me in carpet to wait in the basement, cobwebs in streaks in the sunlight that penetrated the small windows. Though I begged him to hide with me, he left. "I must," he declared, pointing to the fight. What final words! "Must" is the word that brought his death. Gunfire swirled around the house, and acrid smoke filled the air. I turned my head to the cool stone, invoking the old hymn: "Rock of Ages cleft for me, Let me hide myself in Thee." I hid in rock, my eyes locking on limestone, the chalk of this region, so fit for building. "Our foundation," Solomon had said, "so why not our first-story walls? More to be built later." In that rock, I saw shapes. The rock was not so much rock as it was home to a thousand lines, etchings, lacings, small white curves like cut fingernails, dots like sand carried onto the floor by careless boots, little twigs and stems like the litter left by birds under the cherry tree. These shapes in the Rock of Ages had before now been hidden to my eyes.

Why do I write of this instead of what came next? The terrible silence, followed by the mournful wailing of women and children. The escape from carpet and foundation, the ascent toward death. I ran to Solomon. Above his body stood a man, dragoon pistol in one hand, with a patchy beard and drunk red eyes as he leered at me, his free hand suddenly producing Solomon's pocket watch. The plunderer jerked at the fob. "No!" I screamed. "You have taken his life. That is enough!" I rushed toward him. I snatched the fob, loosed the watch from the ruffian's hand, and threw myself on Solomon's body. The man raised his gun and cocked the hammer. Then he turned and staggered away.

I dissolved into Solomon's bloody body. When I dared rise, I examined him. Shot not once, but three times—hand, heart, head. This weight was too much for me to bear. I fainted like so many others.

A few survivors carried buckets to my flaming porch, but its roof columns and floorboards could not be saved, and, giving up, two old men took axe to wood and separated the burning structure from the stone house, the open doorway now three feet from the ground. I could not help them. I lay in the dry grass, fires burning around me, and wondered who might douse flames, who might bury the bodies that lay still, who might minister to the tear-stained cheeks of the children, the dead hearts of the women? I lay beside my Solomon and waited, my eyes closed, the shapes embedded in the foundation rocks playing on my eyelids. I cannot remember being revived, I cannot remember when Solomon's body was removed to the Methodist Church, I cannot remember the words spoken—of condolence, commiseration, sympathy, understanding. I remember only the smell of smothering smoke, of fetid blood, of still air, heat laden and dense in my nostrils. In my hand was Solomon's watch, held so tightly that I thought the impression of his initials etched in the casing might never leave the flesh of my palm.

When I finally returned home, I had to fashion a pile of rocks into makeshift stairs in order to climb into what had once felt like a sanctuary. I went immediately down to the foundation and examined the shapes of things in the stone. I could do nothing else.

Diary Entry

Sunday, August 23, 1863

Not so much rock as
computed detritus
shells
bones?

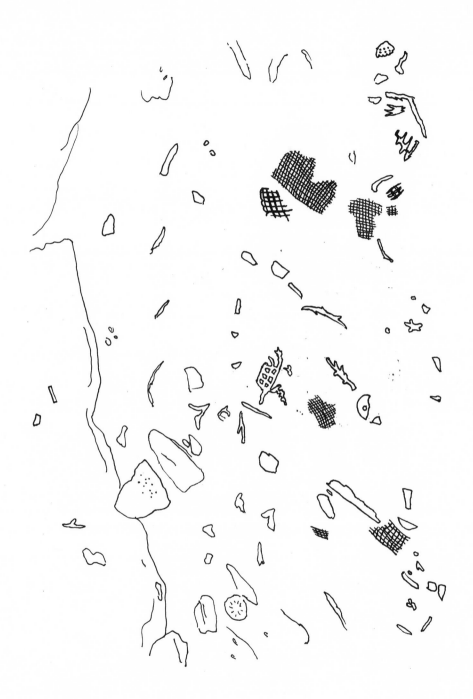

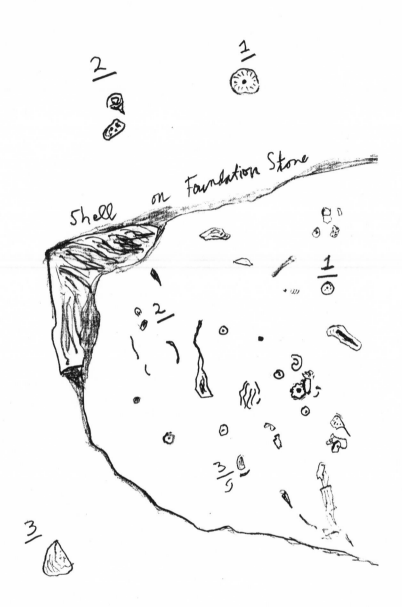

Shell on Foundation Stone

Diary Entry

Monday, September 4, 1863

I watched them hammer the final nail into Solomon's coffin. I watched them heave the box into the wagon bed and cover it with tarp after tarp. I climbed onto the seat next to Mr. Browder and, against all advice, we set off for the long journey to Pine Bluff, Arkansas, my girlhood home and his boyhood haunt, now occupied, thankfully, by Union troops.

The miles, the hours, the days, the heat, and finally the stench doubled the burden of our travel. Never was corpse more ready for grave, for we skirted population, south through Kansas, into Indian Territory, entering Arkansas close to the Ouchita River. We followed the water to Hot Springs, where Union troops had defeated Confederate, and from there we traveled only at night to Union-occupied Pine Bluff. When encountered, we called Solomon "cousin" or "family friend." This made our errand seem one of casual mercy rather than of terrible need, for all needs are suspect and give enemies advantage. Soon enough, of course, none would come close enough to inquire. We buried Solomon Doerr's remains where he will remain, above a sparkling creek among pines, water gurgling, birds singing, though nothing could placate my heaving heart nor stop my tears. Mr. Browder left me behind where I might find succor among family.

Mother and Father Doerr have begged me to stay with them. Perhaps that would relieve them of their own emptiness. Surely I am not certain how I can fill myself back up. All that we hoped for is gone, I thought, and it was true throughout the journey and the burial. Solomon was gone, the kind and dedicated man with whom I had hoped. But the hope of Kansas, the good people who had kept slavery from the territory, who had made Kansas a Free State— that hope and those people were not gone. Father Robert and Mother Jo, Mary and John, Hiram and Penelope all have room for me in their homes should I want to stay, but much calls me back to my new home. I am unsure where I belong, or where I long to be.

For now my affairs are unsettled in Lawrence. I have my small stone home. I have claims on property in the town. I have my friends and my church. I have the mystery of rock to solve. Tomorrow I take Sport, a good, fast horse, and ride toward Lawrence. Father Robert will ride with me for my safety, though I hardly care, for what more could beset me than I have already experienced?

I could take refuge in Arkansas. Certainly the Doerrs would care for me, as would my family. Certainly my nieces and nephews would provide me hours of comfort, perhaps, after some time, even joy. But what would I be here but a woman who has suffered tragedy? Refuge is different from future. Sanctuary is not only comfort and safety, but a way of hiding. If a life is spent hiding, a life cannot be seeking. I plan to seek. When Father Robert and Mother Jo found me in the arms of my dead mother, my father murdered, they gave me refuge and sanctuary. They also taught me to stand up, to learn, to make my dead parents proud.

Solomon's last words inspire me. "I must!" I must return to Lawrence. I must fulfill my life and my hopes there. I must honor my Solomon, and my Benjamin and my Lawrence, my two lost boys. I must travel through dangerous territory to return to what I must call home. I must find myself.

Diary Entry

I was in my foundation, candlelight supplementing the meager sunlight that pene-
trated the two small rectangular windows cut in the walls, working, as I had been
for each spare minute I could find, with hammer and chisel, chipping out the small
bits of life I had discovered, separating them from foundation stone for study.

Winnie Terrant climbed the makeshift stone steps and entered my home, her
church shoes clattering the floorboards above me. "Nell," she called. She paced the
floors through the drawing room and kitchen. The back door opened and closed,
then her steps again, this time just above me. "Nell," she called again. "Nell Doerr,
wherever are you!"

I struck the joists with my hammer, and Winnie screamed. I struck again, for
the blows against the wood helped me spend my frustration and anger. "Nell, is
that you?" Winnie shouted.

"Indeed!" I shouted.

She came to the trap door in the corner, which evidently she had not seen ajar,
and up I climbed, musty, dirty, cobwebbed. I sneezed in the sunlight. Winnie was
still pale from the fright I had given her with the hammer, and of course I was a
frightening sight as well, my oldest dress mussed, no shoes on my feet. I held a
stone in one hand, the hammer and a chisel in the other, and she backed away
from me as though I were a Missouri savage. She retreated to the door and held
up her hands. "We haven't seen you," she said. "You've been hiding? Nell, you do
not need to be afraid. Lawrence is secure. We are protected." She spoke calmly,
steadily, as though trying to calm a frightened child.

I laughed. I set my specimen and tools on the dining table and sat as primly as
possible. "Winnie, I am not hiding. I am seeking. Mad as I must look, I am fine. I
am busy."

"You're not coming to church?" she asked quietly.

"No," I said. "I must make use of daylight. For my studies."

"Your studies?"

I swept my arm across the table, where lay my several rows of fossils, sorted by shapes. I know nothing now but shapes: round buttons, shell-like striations, white lace, bones or shells perforated with dots, spine-like ridges, waving fans. I was exhausted suddenly, looking at the ten days of work. "I can't go out," I said. I closed my eyes, the strain of finding minute creatures rendering them nearly useless. Or perhaps I was hiding sudden tears.

Winnie approached and took my rough hand in her soft ones. "We need you in church. I'll help you clean up."

I let her. Presentable, we went to church, a sea of widows in black dresses radiating darkness. I thought of my foundation space, my sputtering candle, my moments of discovery. Oh, Solomon, certainly that is all I know of hope on this Lord's day, five weeks your widow.

Diary Entry

Today would have been your thirty-eighth birthday, Solomon Doerr. In 1840 you were a gangly fifteen, all knuckles and elbows. Every time you set to a meal, you ate as though the time had come to fill yourself out and become a man. Your father, who had business several times a year with mine, was of the same build, and of the same appetite. We fed you, Mother and I, and the ones you brought, secreted in the wagon, those poor souls with the keenest appetites for food and for freedom.

I, too, was fifteen, taller and heavier than you, already filled out as a woman, and suddenly come to your attention. After supper we went together to the barn to prepare the small basement room for our wayfarers: water for washing, clean straw, blankets, a basket of apples.

You were shy of speech but boundless in energy. As we came from underground you spotted the rope, hanging from the topmost rafter of the barn. You climbed the ladder to the loft, unwound the rope from the loft beam, and shouted, "Bet you never saw a flip swing. Solomon Doerr special." You held the rope in both hands, ready to launch yourself from the loft floor into the great cavern of the open barn.

"Solomon," I yelled at you. I jumped up and down. I held up both hands. But I was too late.

You thought I was protesting what you knew to be a daredevil stunt. "I must show you!" And you swung from the loft.

"The pulley," I screamed, my horror turning into another scream as the rope went taut and engaged the pulley, which slid on the track you had not seen, directly into the closed barn door, where you hit, feet in the air, ready to flip, I suppose. You landed like a sack of potatoes, face first into the threshold, blood gushing from your broken nose.

I raced to you and cradled your thin body in my arms. I kissed your forehead

over and again. You opened your eyes. You smiled widely. "Look before you leap,"
you said, shaking your head.

"I did," I said, kissing your smiling lips, my heart performing its own flip
swing.

If only your eyes had opened. If only your lips could have smiled up at me, as I
held you, blood leaking from the bullet to your temple, the blast to your chest. My
heart is a dull thud. Everything that brought us to Kansas also conspired to kill
my Solomon Doerr.

The heart must be broken, cracked open, before we understand what is inside.
Grief resides there, but grief is not the sole contents of the heart—the gems of life
and curiosity also lurk there, waiting to be embraced.[*]

---

[*] This undated note on the back of the previous page, perhaps an afterthought, seems quickly scrawled, or perhaps written in darkness.

Diary Entry

My first time on the river. A short walk north and east, until I could climb down the bank onto a sandbar. The sky was its bluest, the cottonwood and sycamore leaves beginning to shade into yellows and browns, the grasses riverside, rusting. On a sandbar all is quiet. The birds leave their calls on the riverbank, the river itself is sluggish and meandering. My footsteps are muffled in the packed sand, squishy where the loose sand pushes up rock, small and worn, but full of fossils.

This river is so unlike even the smallest creek in Arkansas, where water is always in a hurry to get to its destination, where it is clear rather than muddy, where it loves the sound of itself against rock, against fallen tree. Here the wood is driftwood, and even "drift" seems an exaggeration. Perhaps it is stalled wood, stuck wood, abandoned wood that only moves with the next downpour, when the river lifts itself into activity. That activity exposes what I look for.

I bent to my work, hunching along the sand, looking for rock with the impressions of former life stamped into it. Those were the fossils I'd seen in the foundation of my house. And there were what looked like teeth and bones. But I did not expect to find what looked like twigs, like stems, like the pieces of the bodies of some creature, small and delicate as a plant, the branching stone sometimes pocked with holes so fine they looked to be perforated. They were part of something that once lived in these waters—as river or, as I have read, ancient ocean, I must know—and I began to look only for them, some branched into the shape of a "Y," others tapered and ridged as though they were screws. I placed my finds in a bag, along with some clam and snail shells for the ornamentation of my bare rooms. Though the larger finds interested me, and I knew I would

come to understand their place in the eons of our world, the smaller creatures—
delicate, spineless, nearly invisible at first, attracted my most willful attention.
I must find someone to look at what I've discovered on this quiet day, the first
day I have forgotten myself, walking alone, maybe the last creature on this
earth, connected only to what I could find, could gather, could take back into the
living world of Lawrence, Kansas.

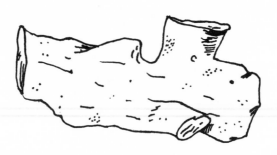

These early discoveries are not labeled, but they seem, from top to bottom,
to be closest to Fistulipora, Archimedes, and Stomatopora.

Letter to Sister Mary

Sunday, October 18, 1863
Lawrence, KS

Dearest Mary—

Sometimes I talk to you aloud in my house, pacing, as I do, through sleepless nights. Though it is two months after the onslaught perpetrated by the Confederate guerillas, Lawrence is still dressed in black, two months of black, of widow's weeds, black armbands worn by the surviving males. We cannot, nor do we want to, forget our grief. Husbands and sons ripped from our homes, from the embraces of wives and mothers, and shot, point blank, by Quantrill's raiders, until 157 lay dead.

You remember how Solomon secreted me in the foundation of our home, and went for his gun, but in hiding me he was slowed, and his slowness surely cost him his life, for he was barely to the street when shot. I heard the shot that killed him. I will always hear that shot. Pistol cracks and rifle shots and shotgun blasts. In Arkansas, just after you were born, ice pelted our farm and coated the trees that surrounded our fields. After the storm a remarkable quiet accompanied a dazzling sun. In that quiet, tree limbs stuttered, shattered, cracked, and popped, dropping to the ground like dead men. My heart iced just so after Solomon was shot, and Lawrence's heart iced just so that fateful morning, and we all feel limbless, separated as we are from our men. These months we have huddled in mourning, vulnerable, as though awaiting yet another storm.

Mary, our churches pick the darkest hymns. No more marching through "A Mighty Fortress is our God." Though our ministers preach comfort, they cannot comfort. Though they speak of finding ourselves, of finding strength, most are lost. You have no doubt read President Lincoln's Proclamation. Tomorrow we will gather in this first official day of giving thanks. I copy the lines that strike me as reprinted in the *Journal*, "to set apart and observe the last Thursday of November next as a day of thanksgiving and praise to our beneficent Father who dwelleth in the heavens. And I recommend to them that while offering up the ascriptions justly due to Him for such singular deliverances and blessings they do also, with humble penitence for our national perverseness and disobedience, commend to His tender care all those who have become widows, orphans, mourners, or sufferers in the lamentable civil strife in which we are unavoidably engaged, and fervently implore the interposition of the Almighty hand to heal the wounds of the nation and to restore it, as soon as may be consistent with the divine purposes, to the full enjoyment of peace, harmony, tranquility, and union." You know I went to hear Lincoln, as he was readying himself for the presidency. I can hear his voice in those words.

We have celebrated Thanksgivings before, of course, the New Englanders having brought the tradition with them from Massachusetts. But our president has made this an official day, and for us it will be one of equal parts thanks and grief, I must confess to you. Although we gather in our churches and are sheltered in our sadness, often I walk alone. Then, I am not grieving, I am finding. Nearly everywhere, my eyes, downcast, are brightened with joy.

You will remember that, in the foundation space where Solomon bade me lie down, where he covered me with carpet, I rested my head against the cool limestone. In that stone were the shapes of tiny creatures, once living, now fossilized. Kansas teemed with such sea creatures, as I have read, and their lives, made permanent in rock, have begun to give me new life.

I find I must be outdoors. I resent the stiff, black dresses. As when we were girls in Arkansas, I long to venture, unaccompanied, into woods, onto bluffs, into the river, and to the sandbars. Sometimes I am gone all day—to the scandal of all—and come home with a satchel heavy with rocks that contain evidence of the life of long ago. I have hired men to carry my treasures, and dressed more the part of adventuress than of widow.

"You are like a bird," said Margaret Littlefield, the minister's wife. "You flit. You seem almost gay." She had brought three other women with her, enough to give her more force in her disapproval. "These stones you expect our men to carry for you, what do you intend to do with them?"

They wore veils over their lovely faces, Mary, just as they expected me to wear. But in a veil I cannot see. I cannot discover. I cannot discern. "I will study them," I said. "They are my specimens."

"Specimens?" asked Olivia Johnson, examining me as though *I* were *hers* to study.

"That's exactly what I told you she calls her stones," said Winnie Terrant.

"Have you read Darwin?" I asked the church ladies.

They stood to leave. Now I wear black only in church. Sundays remain a comfort. On that day I am accepted into a circle of mourning.

The rest of the week I work in silence, with no companions, bent toward discovery.

I thank God that I can write these thoughts, contradictory as they must seem, for I grieve and discover new things in equal measure. Write to me soon, my dear Sister.

Your loving Nell

Probate Notice and Land Sales

"What was to be ours, a life together lived long and well, has now become mine. Even in death you have provided. Your providence means that all that was ours, except for our humble home and my humble self, will pass to others so that I might be free from want. All but the want of you."[*]

---

[*] Nell's valise of documents and artifacts contains probate records and several bills of sale, dating to the late fall and winter of 1863–1864, the months after Quantrill's Raid. During a time when Lawrence was eager to rebuild—so that the signs of desolation might be erased—Nell evidently profited handsomely from Solomon Doerr's claims on land and lots close to the center of Lawrence. Research shows that property values rose dramatically, and, in a letter to the probate court, Nell pressed to have all of Solomon Doerr's properties ceded to her name, as required by law after a husband's death. A probate notice from the *Daily Kansas Tribune* (Lawrence, KS) of December 2, 1863, shows Nell's intentions to sell the properties. Nell evidently used the firm of Hendry & Akin as broker for the sales of her lots.

Little mention is made of these financial transactions in her diary; only one plaintive, undated entry speaks to her relief in being provided for when so many Lawrence widows were forced to take in boarders or laundry to survive.

Notice

IS HEREBY GIVEN TO THE TAX

Payers of Anderson County, State of Kansas, that th Taxes for 1863 are now due; and the rate per cent is as follows, to wit: State tax, eight and a half mills; County tax, twelve and a half mills; School tax, two and a half mills; Territory tax, one mill; Township tax, one mill; and for the purpose of collecting the same, I will attend the following named places in person, or by Deputy, to wit:

Greeley, Walker township, Friday, Dec. 17.
Esq. Dennis's Jackson township, Saturday, Dec. 18.
Central City, Reeder township, Monday, Dec. 20.
Hyatt, Washington township, Tuesday, Dec. 21.
Elizabethtown, Ozark township, Wednesday, Dec. 22.
Indian Creek, Ozark township, Thursday, Dec. 23.

And at my office in Garnett thereafter; and if the taxes are not paid by the 12th of January, 1864, there will be a penalty of ten per cent. added to the same.

H. CAVENDER, Treasurer.

Nov. 27.—4.w.

Administratrix's Notice.

NOTICE is hereby given that letters of administration have been granted to me upon the estate of Sol. Doerr deceased, late of the county of Douglas, in the State of Kansas, by the Probate Court, within and for said county, dated October 5th. A. D. 1863. All persons having claims against the said estate are required to exhibit the same for allowance to me, within one year after date of said letters aforementioned; or they may be precluded from any benefit of such estate; and if the same be not exhibited, as aforesaid, within three years from the date of said letters, such claims shall be forever barred.

Nell J. Doerr

Administra... of the estate of Sol. Doerr, dec'd.
Lawrence, Noven. 1863. #6-8

Diary Entry

Sunday, August 21, 1864

My dearest Benjamin and Lawrence—

You are ever in my thoughts. You lie at peace, your short lives marked by permanent stone. You would have had your father's bushy eyebrows, your mother's ungainly stature, your Grandfather Robert's sure voice, your Grandfather Peter's fine hands, your Grandmother Jo's nimble intelligence. You would have inherited much to sustain you. You came from people who choose to make a difference, from settlers who settled so that they might unsettle the world—my parents to Arkansas, Solomon's parents freeing human flesh from bondage, your father and I to K.T. to continue the unsettling of slavery in this country. I, too, am unsettled, left as I am in this world of death and war. Out of hopelessness, out of the quiet of my empty house, I can only imagine the life I might have had, and the lives you might have had.

You would have lived with passion; you would have lived with energy. You would have been everywhere at once, and I would have tired trying to keep up with you. I would have put you on a horse at three years old. I would have taught you to swim, your father to whittle and to whistle. We would have pitched into letters, to reading and writing, just as my mother and I learned together well before I grew past her knees.

Your father would have taken you everywhere with him, singing all the songs he knew, playing spoons for rhythm, his tongue clicking, his lips buzzing and popping through "Hole in the Bucket" and "Go Tell Aunt Rhody," with its "The old gray goose is dead, standing on her head." How many are dead, how many taken before their time? How many goslings scratching for bread, crying? How many ganders weeping?

You had no time, yet you live eternally. As long as I have a heart to beat, as long as I have lungs to fill, a head to think, fingers that miss touching you, breasts swollen then shrunken, arms empty with longing—as long as I am myself, you will live. You will live with me, and I with you. You were in your father's heart, and you are forever with him, marked in stone as he is, marked as living, as having lived, marked, marked, and with this, re-marked.

I memorialize you on this day, the anniversary of your father's death.

Your Loving Mother!

Letter to Sister Mary

Monday, December 12, 1864
Lawrence, KS

My dearest Mary—

Sister, when I see myself as others see me, to echo our dear Burns, I come to understand their mixture of emotions—sympathy, pity, fear, scorn, perhaps even horror. I wear my oldest bonnets, sensible boots, my worn dresses all faded brown as a thrush, and, crossing each shoulder, a canvas satchel for the specimens I might find. I am sometimes bent with their weight, so that, stooped, I appear to be begging, my dirty, calloused hands thrust forward. I perspire like any working person, and I fear I emit a most unpleasurable odor (even to myself). Those who once spoke to me avoid my glance, sometimes even move to the other side of the street as they see me approach. I am like a dirty Hester Prynne, with my bright fossils, my discoveries, being my Pearl.

Yes, it has come to this, reckless as I have been with my reputation. Mary, I am no harlot, no fallen woman. I am a widow, not an adulteress. That I walk by myself, unaccompanied by chaperone, man or woman, that I manage my own affairs without seeking the advice of Banker Whitaker, that I observe the world instead of attending church meetings, making nature my sanctuary—these things brand me as somehow fallen.

Mary, I have fallen—to earth, to rock, to the elements, to a future of scientific comprehension of the universe, heaven enough for me. My falling makes others afraid. For what if they became like me—beset by the inspiration that comes with the incomprehensible? What would they lose? Propriety? Standing? Stature? Community?

I have lost so much already. Two perfect babies before their ripening; my Solomon; the front of my home to fire, just as my first parents' home was torched by violent men. I nearly lost my will to live except as I might come to understand my fossils. Perhaps this loss makes me so bent on discovery, on finding.

Winnie Terrant has remained my friend. Sadie Gilbert will dine with me outside the presence of her husband, and he travels a great deal, so we share meals often enough, and she is good company. Olivia Johnson invites me weekly to weak tea. Miss Lydia Stone has asked me, privately, to read Darwin with her. Mary, this may sound like a lament, but please know that I do not consider myself lamentable.

Your loving sister, Nell

Diary Entry

I did not attend church services today. I do not know whether my discomfort is in my mental conflict with church doctrine—what few tenets we Unitarians maintain to begin with—or with the way I am spoken to, questioned, and shown concern as though I were an invalid. My interest in science is not a disease, not a condition of the mind that needs curing.

Groups do not like to include those who are thinking or behaving differently from expected. No wonder they question me. Unfortunately, I do not answer well. I do not know what to expect from myself, just as they cannot predict what I might say or do. I suspect myself as the church ladies suspect me. Perhaps their discomfort with me too closely mirrors my discomfort with myself.

I will stay away for a time. I will see how severing that obligation changes my perspective about religion, science, and myself. When Winnie asked whether I feared choosing Science over Religion, I could not tell her that one doesn't choose one over the other if one can hold both within mind and heart. Fear powers those most upset with Darwin and scientific theory. Churches are alarmed that a new idea might push out old habits of mind, old comforts, old assumptions. The true scientific mind—one that questions, one that collects evidence, one that frames theories and tries to prove—seems harsh and cold to many. I am trying to learn that mind, to have that mind, exacting with myself and what I am discovering in the world.

In the process I do not want to lose my heart, my feelings, my wonder, my awe. I admit that I do have more awe for what I discover in the natural world than what I can merely speculate to be a heaven or an afterlife. I have had enough afterlives to last me through my mortal time—after leaving family, after losing children, after losing Solomon. The loss of those lives is still a heavy burden, made harder for me to bear as I become isolated. The church has comforted me in those things, yes, soothing me like a mother soothes a crying baby. Perhaps what I seek now is my own true self, not my suffering, comfort-needing heart that is indeed so like a baby. I seek instead the passionate will of a woman, matured and able to nurture herself.

I confuse myself even as I write to clarify my thinking. These pages, re-read, do nothing to illuminate. They state, though, what I will and will not do. There, Nell, you've written it down clearly. Now follow your own direction.

Diary Entry

Benjamin Mudge, recently appointed a professor at the State Agricultural College, is to address the Congregational church tomorrow evening. As the newspaper wrote, urging all to attend, "The earth's history for millions of years, is written in the rocks that surround it, and yet, most of the intelligences that walk its surface, are as ignorant of this history as the mole that creeps under it."

I was a mole myself just but a few years ago. I hope to be one of the intelligences; I'm certain I would thrill to his lecture. Yet I think of Mudge, recognizing me in the audience, and approaching, and asking after Mr. Dorfman—the name Solomon always used on his excursions with contraband—and I reconsider. I must not go. For it was the same Benjamin Mudge who, but four years ago, secreted Missouri slaves who had made the dangerous crossing to Quindaro. He told Solomon of his taking in these particular slaves—a woman and three children—and even defending them against men who sought after them for their master. Mudge was not afraid of threats, and stood his ground, shotgun in hand one night, then remained at the ready for two days before we could arrive. Had he known that Mudge's contraband was so openly held, Solomon might not have allowed me to accompany him. The woman's name was Maryemma. Her three children, eleven, nine, and seven, were Henry, Martha, and James. They were eager for the transport to Leavenworth, though it was February, and cold, with snow flurries as we loaded them into Solomon's wagon, all fitted as it was with cabinets, those on the top and sides filled with the tools of the carpenter's trade, fitting given that Solomon felt he was doing the Lord's work, and wasn't Jesus a carpenter? Underneath the cabinets were the enclosures in which the woman and her children must secret themselves for what would be an uncomfortable, close-quartered, bumping, rumbling journey. I know, because I rode under the

46

cabinetry more than once, the first time to gain empathy for our human cargo, the others because Solomon perceived danger.

How well I remember Mr. Mudge, his wife and two sons. They had certainly had a courageous several days defending Maryemma and her children from capture and transport back across the Missouri River, so they were as relieved as the slaves for the next leg of their journey. We arrived in a day and a half. At night Maryemma helped me with the fire and the preparation of our food—she was a clever and good-natured woman who sang songs quietly and continually, as though the sound of her voice might keep all calm, might keep her flight to freedom in motion.

I do not know, as we rarely ever knew, what became of Maryemma. I do know what became of Solomon Doerr, and Mr. Dorfman with him. I do know what has become of me, widow, now studying rock for signs of ancient life. Would Mudge recognize me, and ask me to explain my presence? Could I bear the lie I might tell, or the confession I might make? Could I speak calmly of those years, given Solomon's murder, to a man who escaped murder though he shared the same cause?

I am fraught. I am overwrought. Rather than answer such questions, rather than risk having to answer them, I will not attend the lecture, though I see myself hiding, like contraband in the bottom of the wagon, still waiting for my freedom to go, to learn, and to think as I please.

Diary Entry

Samuel Winston. I did not expect a man so young, though he is newly studying at the university, after being trained by Mudge at the Agricultural College. Professor Snow thought it necessary to have someone who might build a collection for the University's cabinet of rocks, minerals, and fossils. Winston is both student and teacher.

I had to bend slightly to shake his hand, and I wondered if he thought me an Amazon. He invited me into his office, and enjoined me to take a seat, but I could not. I had first to examine this wonder of a place, desks and shelves stacked with books, with minerals, with fossil rocks, bones, and butterflies. Stuffed birds. A raccoon and several snake skins. Leaves and a squirrel skeleton. "My cat," Winston said, pointing to the one live animal, black furred, with green eyes staring down at me in a sphinx of a pose. "Hypothesis," he said, and the cat meowed. How unlike the cat was Samuel Winston. The man was more bird, moving quickly, gesturing each word as though pecking it from his mouth, perching, finally, on a chair. I sat opposite him, and from my satchel took the few fossils I'd brought to show him. He set them upon his desk, removed a magnifying glass from a shelf, and studied the wispy remains. I wondered what he saw.

He looked up finally, holding the magnifying glass in the air, one eye large behind it. "Bryozoan," he said, and smiled. "Part of a fenestella. And this . . ." he gestured for me to stand beside him, holding the glass above another piece of fossil, ". . . this looks to be a bit of phyllopora." The glass was out of focus for me. "Higher," I said, and reached for his hand to raise the glass. He did not flinch at my touch, though even my gloved hand felt the warmth of his. Was this untoward? "How will I ever learn these names?" I asked him.

"As everyone learns them," he said, releasing the glass to my hand. "Through study."

"And what should I be looking for?" I asked him.

"You have more than these?" he asked.

"Many," I said.

"Then find more, even more. Bring them to me each week at this time. We will learn what you have, and learn what you might look for. Not everyone is so interested in these as you seem to be."

"They seem to be everywhere," I confessed. I almost babbled, bubbling as I was with his knowledge and his praise that I had found something valuable, but I had already taken his time, and he had already arranged a time when I might return. "I must learn," I said. "I must have something to read. Something of science."

He looked past me to his shelves of books. "Darwin's Origin?" he asked.

"I have read it. Many times."

"Indeed," he said. He flitted to the shelf and brought down a rather large tome. "Have you read Whewell? William Whewell? This was published just a few years ago." Winston read the title dramatically, "On the Philosophy of Discovery: Chapters Historical and Critical." He showed me the title page, on which one hand is passing a torch to another. Then he turned the pages. "This chapter, 'Philosophy of Discovery.' You will appreciate it. Whewell was the first to call us scientists." He found the page he wanted and read, "'Sciences begin by a knowledge of the laws of phenomena, and proceed by the discovery of the scientific ideas by which the phenomena are colligated, as I have shown in other works. The discovery of causes is not beyond the human powers, as some have taught.'

"Let us collaborate in your discoveries." Samuel Winston shut the book and handed it to me. Thick and heavy. I exited into the hall, but found my young teacher soon at my side. "You must document," he demanded, "as exactly as you can. Place and date and time. We will find a section map. Have you a timepiece? Can you recollect the details of your other discoveries?"

"I will do my best," I said.

I enjoyed every step home, heavy tome in my arms, knowing that soon its words would become something I could also carry in my mind. I saw Solomon's pocket watch in my desk drawer, waiting to be of daily use once more. Time seemed to move more quickly, as did I, eager to document, hungry to read, impatient for our meeting next week.

Diary Entry

Among the books lent me by Samuel Winston is The Rocks of Kansas, *by
G. C. Swallow and F. Hawn. To think that they were studying samples of rock,
Swallow from a distance and Hawn on the ground, and publishing this first
record in 1858, a mere eight years ago. To think that science was being written
about and from the very place I live, and I then with so little awareness of science. To think that these men, fledglings in the geography and topography and
geology of Kansas, were already arguing science. In their book Swallow and
Hawn note the existence of Permian rocks in Kansas, which greatly excited a
Mr. Meek, who supposed he had the right to announce what he called an "exclu-
sive discovery." Hawn certainly makes a passionate defense of his and Swallow's right to publish their examination of Kansas fossils and, with it, the claim
of the Permian. Of course, I gain this perspective through hindsight, and
through my tutorials with Samuel, dear man that he has already become to me.*

*I won't say to Samuel my true thoughts, that none of their bickering is science
in the least. Unless, that is, someone might study the science of how animals protect their lairs, how men fight over their claims, as early settlers so often did in
K.T. These men might spend their time better in pursuit of fossils, and not of fame.
Someday, perhaps, we will all know more than either of them knows now. Meek,
indeed! Sometimes the admission of ignorance, the admission that all is speculation, would be most appropriate. Spoken like a woman, I chastise myself. Will I
someday know science well enough to question others, to make claims, to make a
difference?*

*Samuel thinks so, or so he tells me. He keeps me and my studies with him a
kind of secret. "What would Mudge say, were he to know I've taken you on as
student, when his expeditions are exclusively male, and the sturdier men the*

better. I hardly qualified for such rigorous exploration myself," Samuel said, *"as slight as I am."*

"No one would call me slight," I said to him, my view on the top of his head. He looked up from his desk and smiled.

"If you ever meet Mudge," he said, *"be certain you are seated."* He laughed. *"You would not want to intimidate the man!"*

Samuel is right. I do not set out to intimidate any man. But if I did, I would not want it to be through my physical stature, but through the power of my observations and discoveries.

Letter from Brother Hiram

Thursday, January 31, 1867
Pine Bluff, AR

Sister—

I write to you to with news. Jacob Johnson came crying into this world one week ago during a bad ice storm that kept Midwife Red Feather from helping. She needn't have been there with Penelope—she is tough and strong as you know. Are you surprised by another nephew? We were, too, conceiving at our age. His sisters will no longer be interested in their dolls, I suspect. Jacob is quiet, for a baby. Not like me. How did you tolerate my nonsense? A wild animal had more sense than me. When I was always making you chase me horseback. How many times did you climb a tree to coax me down when I went so high and then froze with fear at the top? You let me squeeze your arm so hard those times Mama stitched cuts. You must still have those bruisings.

You were my comfort in sickness. That fever almost sent me to the Lord. Five days your cool hand held mine. Mama told you to rest. You told her you would sleep when my fever broke. You brought cold rags. You sang to me. I still hear that voice—were you thirteen and I was nine or ten? Your voice still pulls me up when I feel low. I wish I might send that voice back to you. Do you sing? Perhaps in church? I remember your voice, next to mine, filling our little sanctuary. I have missed you, Sister Nell.

I have not seen you these years since you brought Solomon home to bury. Are you still dressed in widow weeds? Mary told me you walk along the river there. Sandbars? Bluffs? Looking for rocks with fossils in them. I have heard of that, old creatures turned into rocks like the stone wood we used to find in our Arkansas dells. I hope you are well. I wish you would come and meet your new nephew Jacob. Maybe seeing the living would help you forget the dead.

I spoke with Mary and Michael, and Mama and Papa. We will pay for your passage. Come for a week or two, or longer. You will be comfortable. Your nephews and nieces are eager for you. You know Penelope's reputation as a cook. We have one fat lamb, and duck and venison. My innards grumble writing to you. Come to us, Sister, if you are able.

Your loving brother, Hiram

Letter to Brother Hiram

Saturday, February 16, 1867
Lawrence, KS

Dear Brother—

My heartfelt welcome to little Jacob. May he wax into a strong and capable boy, then into the fine man I know he will be, for he will take after his father. I discern and even appreciate your concern for me. Yes, I will visit, but not until the weather improves. But when the weather improves, I will likely be hunting my dear fossils, so perhaps next fall?

I am fine. My search for fossils is not a sign of a grieving, demented mind, as you seem to think. Instead, after the loss of Solomon, my scientific pursuits—I am reading, studying, learning, and discovering all I can about the ancient creatures that inhabited this same place I now walk every day— are solace. I know that I walk upon layer above layer of life, and that supports me.

Sometimes I wish I had known as a girl what I know now. I could have trained my increasingly practical eye on the rocks, bluffs, and stream beds of Arkansas, where fossils are also being discovered. Life is a queer thing, Hiram. Each time we gain knowledge we see in a new way entirely. The world opens up to us. Were you a practitioner of this new art of photography, can you imagine how you might suddenly perceive light and dark, shadow and substance? I know you to be, like our father, a man studied in horses. When you travel to town, when you see horses in their corrals and pastures, when you see them lining up on the track to race, you know and see all. You know what others do not, what some cannot, and you take your satisfaction in that. So it is with my fossils. Yes, I must seem to some to be touched in the head. Perhaps I am. I am touched by a new way of looking, of seeing, and of knowing. I am a child again, learning the world, building the world, a new world, for myself.

Do not think my absence from you and Mary and Mother Jo and Father Robert to be a willful disregard of family. I have been busy with probates and land sales, creating for myself, out of the claims Solomon filed, a secure life so that I might apply myself to new pursuits. Though, like you, perhaps, some do not quite understand me in my "touched" state, I still have dear acquaintances. Yes, I still sing, though not in church services. In nature I lift my voice to heaven even while my thoughts are on the eons that have grounded me and created the ground on which we all walk.

Hiram, you helped in creating me as well. Our adventures horseback, our discovery of caves, our pursuit of the tallest trees and the deepest swimming holes—all of these things shaped me, as does my love for you and our family. Do not worry about me. I will come for a visit. I will pinch the cheeks of your darling Jacob, and his sisters, and eat well at your table, and challenge you on horseback. I will also bring fossil specimens, and help you see and touch what I see and touch, and am touched by.

Your loving sister, Nell

Diary Entry

My many finds of the bryozoan fossil archimedes seemed to delight Samuel Winston beyond words, for instead of praising the hands of the one who found them, he took my hands in his own. "Nell," he said, "you are a positive genius."

Of course I blushed, though for the compliment or for the touch of his hands I cannot be certain. He dropped my hands and counted my specimens (27). He asked for the page I'd brought noting date, place, and time for each discovery. "I wish all my students had your talent for discovery and notation," he said.

"Then I would be just as any other of your students," I said. Did my face give me away, that I wanted to be singular, that I wanted his praise, his attention?

For he said, "An impossibility," and took my hands in his again. He looked into my eyes, his a deep blue, and shining.

I examined his face, smooth and unblemished, his beard nothing but reddish curls, and I blushed for a second time. I withdrew my large hands, which had warmed in his smaller hands, and he put his thin fingers against his cheeks.

"Yes," he said. "The fossil is named archimedes because of its corkscrew shape, similar to the Archimedes screw invented to carry water. Archimedes was Greek, you know, from the third century BC." Samuel began to pace, filling my head with details of this fenestrate, which formed colonies. He pointed out the rimmed pores so characteristic of this Permian fossil. He became so technical I asked him to slow, so that I might take notes. "Yes," he said, "perhaps I will write something down for you. For next time?"

"Next time?" I asked, unsure why he might be confirming what I had assumed to be a regular appointment.

"You will come back?" His face was flushed. Science had almost helped him recover from emotion.

"Indeed," I said. "And with more archimedes to delight you, no doubt."

I write this unsure of my thoughts and feelings, doubly unsure of Samuel Winston's. But I will not give up my studies.

Letter to Hugh Cameron

Saturday, May 25, 1867
Lawrence, KS

Dear Mr. Hugh Cameron, Brigadier General:

Your letter of May 21 confirms what I have heard from others, that you prefer not to have visitors, no matter how they might respect your personal privacy. As you state, I did visit your property on the afternoon of May 15. That was Thursday, the morning after the violent thunderstorm swept through Lawrence, loosing hail and rain. The mud on my boots confirms my presence and speaks to my mission. You may call me a trespasser, the same that the Lord asked us to forgive.

Perhaps you can forgive my intrusion of your peace if I explain myself. I hope I will not offend you by my reassurance. I care nothing for you, nor for conversation, nor for meddling, nor for carrying gossip to others regarding your standing and current condition. I do care for the unique geography of your land. Situated as you are above the river, among bluffs and outcroppings, with timber and the habitation of many animals, large and small, your land might be a treasure trove of the one thing I find I must pursue: fossils. I am dedicated to the discovery and understanding of the remains of all the life that has preceded us on this earth these thousands—nay, millions—of years.

You may complain of my scientific interests. Many have. I believe all that the great Charles Darwin has written in his brilliant work, *On the Origin of Species*. He describes "missing links." I dedicate myself to the discovery of the ancient record, as manifested in the relatively new country of the West. Forgive my trespass on your land, and perhaps on your philosophy.

I am, Nell Johnson Doerr

Diary Entry

To say that I should not have examined the packet of letters, once found, is to say that I am not human. Like so many of my findings, the packet did not come from search, did not come from a desire to discover, did not come from acute observation. Instead, all else fell away from my vision that afternoon in the woods, and the packet in the hollow of a tree was as obvious to me as a flag on a pole. I flew to it.

Letters in what could only be a woman's flowery cursive were ribboned together, the ribbon bows grimy from being opened and re-tied often. The first several were addressed to "My Dear Hugh," and ended, "I am yours, Priscilla."

All of us know Hugh Cameron, of course, who lives near these woods, and he is nobody's. If he courted Priscilla, nothing came of the relationship. The history of Hugh Cameron, his solitary life, his renaming of himself as the "Kansas Hermit" would be contained in the final letter, or so I guessed, and so I read, having turned to that sheet as easily as I found the packet. I am but human, a human who does not always seek, but always finds.

A letter of farewell, no matter how heartfelt, is a heartless thing, and I felt shame after reading those final words: "I cannot, and will not, come to you, cannot and will not share my life with you, having warred too long between what my heart feels and my head tells me, fearing a confusing courtship will bring nothing but a confusing life. I seek settlement, to be settled. For all you have to offer, you cannot, I know, offer me that. Adieu."

Diary Entry

"You sneaked into my letters," said Hugh Cameron, appearing atop a bluff along the river, where I'd gone after last night's storm. Erosion reveals the fossils I seek so diligently. I looked up at Mr. Cameron, his dark form blocking out the setting sun.

"They were in that tree, for anyone to see."

"Seeing is not reading," he said.

"I did not read them," I said.

"You lie," he said, and sat down. His boots dangled close to my shoulders, where I stood examining the limestone outcropping.

"I do not tell the entire truth. I did not read them. I glanced. I read the last letter." Confession made us equals, and so I added, "I am so sorry."

"I do not need your sympathy," Hugh Cameron said. He let himself drop the five feet to stand next to me. He put out a long finger and touched the rock. A perfect fossil specimen appeared under his tapered index. I could barely keep from gasping.

"I am so sorry for reading the letter," I said. "Not for what ensued from the letter I read. I will not be responsible for what you have done, only for what I have done."

"Then you are unlike so many other creatures in this place," said Hugh Cameron. "What do you call this?" he asked, his finger gently reading the white lace of rock. "I see them everywhere."

"It is a bryozoan fossil, and you have found a perfect zooid. I would like to dig it from the rock."

"Yes, you must have everything you find. That is your way, I suppose. This fossil. The knowledge of my letters. To find is to have." He took his finger from the rock.

"I hope you will let me search this bluff. Have I found a fellow explorer in you?" I asked.

"A fellow creature, certainly, for like me you have a mind of your own. Once this was a premium in K. T. But not always appreciated in this fledgling state of Kansas."

I promised to return, and he did not object.

Letter to Sister Mary

Saturday, August 10, 1867
Lawrence, KS

Dearest Mary—

For some time I have known that most of my fossil finds, fragments as they seem to be, might also be pieces of something larger. Do you remember, when we were girls, how often we might happen upon a trash pit at the top of some draw, and find small pieces of crockery? We knew not whether the small triangle, the shiny half moon, the chipped star, was part of a dish, cup, bowl, or pot.

So it has been with my fossils. They have been mere remnants of something unknown, even unimaginable, to me. But through persistent study and direction from Samuel Winston, a student who also teaches at the university, a man who knows much more than I ever will, I have learned that many of my discoveries are parts of a large class of creatures, sea creatures, called bryozoans. They are colonies, and each cell, coming together, differentiates itself into constituent parts of what becomes a creature. Bryozoans attach themselves to the ocean floor and stem themselves up. Some form fanlike, lacy, waving feeders that eat nutrients in the water that are too small for us to even see. In doing so they filter the rich sea water for their sustenance. Like many creatures, the moss bryozoans have mouths, stomachs, and anuses. They have ovaries and testes both, completing their structures and their procreation into the future. They are simply complex, and some, in salty seas, like the one that covered Kansas, calcify for protection. I find the calcified remains, or pieces of them. Perhaps someday, as I build my acumen, I shall find an entire moss bryozoan specimen, a very distant prospect because of their delicacy, their ease in breaking apart. But they are whole creatures, made up of differentiated cells, and they form communities, colonies, together. Imagine them, Mary, an entire bed of them, attached to the ocean floor, waving, fanning the sea current, surviving in richness for years. In fact I have learned that they are not extinct, like so many other fossil forms. Bryozoans live all over the world, having adapted to salt and fresh water. They are still filtering the oceans and seas, still finding life in the simplest and most complicated habitats of the earth. Would that I could see a live bryozoan someday, though I doubt it possible. I enclose a drawing so that you might enjoy, as I do, this remarkable creature.

Your sister, Nell

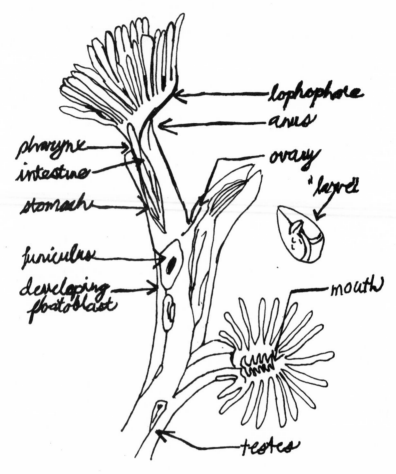

Nell would have copied this drawing of a moss bryozoan from a book.

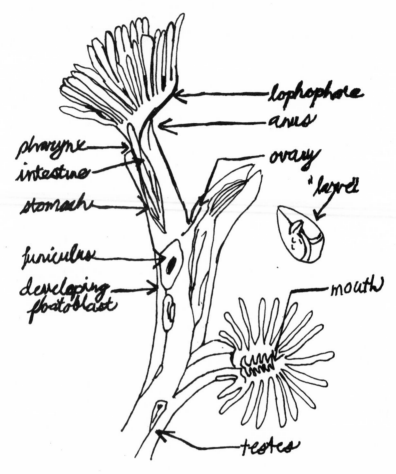

EDITOR'S NOTE

Nell was someone who enjoyed crafting her words, and her diaries and letters are frequently written first as rough drafts, then recopied. Because of this habit, many letters she wrote to others survive in the rough draft form. I offer you an excerpt, to show her writing process: the first paragraph from the document "Letter to Sister Mary, Saturday, August 10, 1867," which she began to draft on August 9.

Diary Entry

*On this eve of departure from Pine Bluff for Lawrence, I must admit Hiram was
right. To be embraced by the arms of those who love you best. To sit at table and feel
as though you never have to push yourself away. To sleep in the bed of your childhood, freshly ticked and crisp, your mother's voice calling you for morning coffee.*

*Then to be awakened at Hiram's house by voices hushed enough for decorum,
but eager for you to join them. Them. What wonders they are. Josephine a wom-
anly seventeen; Antoinette just thirteen; Joyanne, true to her name at ten years
old—she laughs and cries with the same tears, the same shaking of her petite head.
And little Jacob, just born in January—nearly a year old, with his mother's green
eyes and father's chiseled chin, looking a comical version of a man among his dot-
ing sisters.*

*I brought them fossils, one for each of them. The older girls were fascinated as I
tried to explain what fossils were, and why they had different shapes—fenestella
like a fan, stomatopoda with its branches, fistulipora like a root. They wanted
immediately to scour their farm for signs of the lives of the past. Of course their
hopes propelled them outdoors in a stiffly cold wind, and helped them persist along
the creek bank, where water eroded rock, and compelled them to pick up every
stone. Their hands soon chafed. Just as Josephine's enthusiasm waned, Joyanne
found the impression of a shell, then Antoinette a crinoid stem. Josephine was
irked, as she was used to being the authority among them. "I'm so cold," she said. I
was about to march home when she stooped to a loosened wall of earth. She pulled
out an archimedes, exactly like the one I'd brought for baby Jacob. She beamed.
"Inside," I shouted, and we ran.*

*The girls took their treasures to their mother and father, and all marveled that
such things existed all around them—once noticed, forever to be seen, as I'd told*

Hiram in my letter. "How like Jacob's archimedes is the one Joesphine found," I said. "Let's compare."

We could not find Jacob's fossil, though I was certain I'd put it on the table, out of his reach, as a baby's mouth wants everything inside it. Our search was fruitless, and I was beginning to suspect Josephine. Had she picked it up, perhaps securing it in her sleeve in case she didn't find anything? A sensitive young woman, she read my thoughts. "I didn't take it, if that's what you are thinking!" she pouted, and went up to the loft where the girls slept. "No," I cried after her, but we all heard her, sighing from her bed. Sometime later Jacob awoke from his nap and Penelope went to him to nurse. He reached for his mother. In his fist was the archimedes I'd brought him, clutched tightly all afternoon. When Penelope took it from him, he resisted, and wailed in protest until she gave it back. I climbed the ladder to the loft. Josephine had fallen asleep. In her hand, her archimedes. The young holding the ancient.

I bent to kiss her forehead, and Josephine awoke. She smiled, then remembered the trouble and pouted. "Lucky he didn't swallow it," I whispered to her and clutched her hand that held the fossil. "He grasped it before his nap, and still will not let go."

"He gets all the attention," she whispered.

"And you?" I asked. "Do you get attention? From those outside this house? From young men?"

She blushed.

"You will soon have all the attention you want, and need, and deserve," I said. "I can't wait to meet this lucky young man."

I did, after dinner, as Jonathan Young came to sit at the fire. They were shy together, and so I suppose I babbled too much of my experiences in Kansas, our battles and our sacrifices. His father had fought in the Confederacy. "I would have fought, but the war ended before I was yet fifteen," he said.

"You are lucky," I said. "Many were compelled to take a side. As my Solomon said, 'We kill our brothers that we might show them we are right.' He was tired of conflict even before the war began."

"To the future," Hiram said, turning to Jonathan Young.

"Pa is giving me the forty up north of the draw." He took one of Josephine's hands in his. "I'll be building a cabin soon." He tightened his mouth, as though stopping himself from saying more, but we all knew which young woman he wanted to take to that cabin, and Josephine's smile spoke her willingness.

"Look," she said, and she held out the fossil she clutched in her free hand. "I found this today. An archimedes. Your draw will be full of fossils. I must go there to look."

Jonathan looked confused by the fossil and its name, but he wasn't confused about his prospects with Josephine. "I aim to take you there," he said.

After he left, Josephine floated to bed. I set to this diary, to record what has been a restorative trip to my Arkansas home.

Diary Entry

Trust. Such a simple word, buttressed as it is by those two t's. I trusted Samuel. First with my science, then with my desire to study, then with too much of my life. After Quantrill's raid, after my "salvation in stone," as I came to call it, after my interest bore fruit in some minor fossil discoveries, after my excitement grew beyond what I could hold in my breast, I sought a confidante. A man, for few women I knew then—excluding Lydia Stone—seemed the least interested in the evolutionary science of Charles Darwin. Samuel became that confidante, as he'd studied first at Yale with Professor Marsh, then with Mudge here in Kansas. Once he came to Lawrence at the behest of Professor Snow, he fashioned himself a kind of missionary, and I became one of his first savages to convert. He took that missionary and professorial tone with me, at first somewhat patronizing, paternal—Catholic as he was, that religion rare in a Lawrence dominated by Congregationalists, Methodists, and Unitarians. As for me, I had already given my religion hiatus, while he spent many hours discussing how he might reconcile Genesis *with* On the Origin of Species, *religion with science. He thought my lack of religion to be a way of giving up. "We do not negate our spiritual need with science, we enhance it through wonder," Samuel was fond of saying.*

I had much wonder. He taught me about the theories of fossil life, and he held my interest close to his chest, as I asked, for I knew how those in my circle were reacting to me as a woman of science. Unlike others to whom I had spoken, Samuel applauded my excitement, my eagerness to "understand everything," as I often said in those days. He set aside first one, then two afternoons a week for our colloquies. We met so often that people began, inevitably, to talk about what seemed an untoward interest between a widow and a young bachelor—my forty-one years to his thirty. We met only in his office, so as to be among his collections of rocks and fossils, bones and birds, leaves and insects, minerals and skins. Yet gossip haunted us.

Gossip can beget thoughts, those that I had early in the morning hours, when I wondered if Samuel and I might form just such an attachment as people already presumed. Would I, should I, welcome such thoughts? No, I thought, not at the expense of my passion for science, for discovery. When Samuel and I agreed to meet at the river, such thoughts were not foremost in my mind. The spring rains had flooded the sandbars, then receded, and we knew treasures might await, more easily unearthed because of erosion. We anticipated mastodon bones, shells, fossils, all exposed by the calamities of Kansas weather.

I went unaccompanied, that none would think me to be taking more than my usual morning air. I must admit to an excitement, though, perhaps bred of that whiff of scandal. We met on the river bank several miles west of Lawrence, nearing Lecompton, and waded in the cool water, his pants and my dress soaking, sticking to our bodies. "We are silly looking creatures, indeed," said Samuel. He pitched his tent—"base camp," as he had called it—and retreated inside.

He soon reemerged, in his drawers, folding his pants over the peak of the tent. "You may as well do the same with your dress," he suggested. He went back into the tent.

I stood, damp and cold, my nose running. His voice came low and quite matter-of-fact: "Wasn't this to be a day of discoveries?"

"It has been, indeed," I said, and waded into the river for the shore. For safety. For home and reputation.

I could not imagine at the time why I stopped at the bank of the river. I suppose I had already broken rules of propriety, planning an excursion with Samuel, unaccompanied, unchaperoned. I had already shared my passion for science and for fossils, as well as my eagerness to discover them. He had, no doubt, mistaken one eagerness for another. Had I, as well? I stopped on the riverbank, dress soaked from wading to the sandbar and away, to look back at our tent. His head poked from the flap. "I will not sully you!" he shouted.

"You have already," I shouted back. His wet trousers, draped across the tent, were already sending moisture into the dazzling sunlight of the day. My dress matted to my legs and I sneezed. "My reputation," I shouted back. "What of my reputation?"

"Your reputation will be made through achievement. Through science!" He cupped his hands to his mouth to be heard the better. "By what you accomplish.

Better to make *a reputation than to rely on convention. Do you want always to conform to what small minds think?" He disappeared into the tent.*

I waited. Silence. I felt suddenly abandoned. Yet I was the one abandoning him, and the day of fossil finding, and my chance to prove, with my discoveries, the science that Samuel, and Samuel alone, could articulate so well. What folly to be human. Do we survive because of intention, or because of mistakes? In the natural world, there is not right or wrong, there is only what occurs. The sea creatures I feel so bound to study are either extinct, or still exist in oceans on this globe, but not because of reputation. In fact the bryozoans, huddled together, created community, joined others to become single organisms.

Samuel opened the tent flap, retrieved his trousers, went back in to dress, then came to the edge of the sandbar, a trowel in hand. He bent and dug. "Nell!" he soon shouted, holding up a flat rock the size of his hand. "It is as we suspected."

I waded toward him. His discovery was apology and impetus. We did not speak the rest of the morning; we ranged the river. At midday we took the food we had packed. Then more discoveries ensued, of which . . .*

. . . so much the evidence of the past, so many rocks and bones that I had no idea how we might transport them to Samuel's office, to my home, for study. First, of course, we logged them well.

Samuel had arranged for transport. Two of his students, ruddy boys with wheelbarrows, appeared at dusk. By that time Samuel had taken down the tent, dismantled the two tent poles that had stood like the two t's in trust—holding up everything. With the tent packed, no one might know we'd had a refuge for privacy. These boys would respect their professor's reputation, and perhaps mine. But I was ready at this point to face consequences in order to do my work. There was a divinity in these stones. On this day there is a divinity in me, as well. I will not abandon that for propriety and custom.

---

* Here the diary page is stained and torn, and I have not been able to find the fragment among Ms. Doerr's materials (the torn page is included here). The diary entry ends as below, though the possible content torn away is hinted at in a future entry.

world, there is not right or wrong, there is only what occurs. The sea creatures I was so bound to study are either extinct, or still exist in oceans on this globe, but not because they considered reputation. In fact, the bryozoans, huddled together, created community, joined others to become what could only be described as a single organism.

Samuel opened the tent flap, retrieved his trousers, went back in to dress, then came to the edge of the sand bar, a trowel in hand. He bent and dug. "Nell!" he soon shouted, holding up a flat rock twice the size of his hand. "It is as we suspected."

I walked toward him. His discovery was splay and emptas. We did not speak the rest of the morning; we ranged the river. At mid day we took the food we had packed. Then more discoveries ensued, of which sd

sand is w

bordered

Note from Lydia Stone

To Nell Doerr:

I post this note before a journey for which I give you much of the credit. I have been accepted into Wesleyan College, in Macon, Georgia. You must know how my parents see this as scandal—that is, going south, into Georgia, a staunch part of the Confederacy. Yet my correspondence with the College has brimmed with their interest in educating women in general, and me in particular, most especially supporting my interest in the sciences. Mother and Father disapprove, but I do not disobey in setting out for this adventure, for they have come around to it after much entreaty from me.

You know that your influence has helped me to make this decision, though it was some time ago that we studied Darwin together. You were the first person who showed confidence that my ignorance and my provinciality could be conquered through calm and quiet contemplation of the words before me. I remember you once said, "Lydia, these are words first, then sentences, then paragraphs, then grand ideas. Let us begin with the words!" Gracious, how little I understood of Darwin's words, let alone the great man's ideas when I first encountered them on the page, yet how much I understood after our reflections together as we slowly made our way through *Origin*. I dare say you have gone well beyond that book, and furthered your studies here in Lawrence. I might do the same, but instead I am also influenced by your sense of adventure. As you told me, you journeyed from your home to make a difference in your life and the life of the Nation. I hope to do the same thing, to find myself in a new place, with new worlds to understand and conquer.

Know that I think of you with fond remembrance of our hours spent together. To remember them to you, I wonder if you might take on the care of Jane, the small parrot who has called to you on your visits. She would do well with you, if you will take the trouble of her. If you will answer this note expressing your willingness, I will make sure Mother brings Jane to you after I am gone. As for me, I will repay you now and again with an occasional note to tell you of my progress.

I am, sincerely,
Lydia Stone

Diary Entry

Though highly recommended to me by Samuel as a man who could teach me some-thing more of the fossil record, Dr. Forster is nearly deaf. At our first meeting he sat forward at his desk and held a large horn to his ear. "Speak again," he fairly shouted after each of my utterances, so twice I was forced to ask him to teach me what he could of geology, of the history of the earth, of fossils, and particularly invertebrate fossils, to give me books and other publications that would help me understand the great eons of time that have shaped the earth. Forster was said to have met Charles Darwin and Alfred Wallace as he traveled in his own studies throughout the 1860s. He will be in Lawrence only a brief time, and I am told I am fortunate that he granted me audience. In fact he seemed bemused at my requests, as I would be if Jane, instead of her breathy "Pretty bird," chirped out her desire that I read to her On the Origin of Species *aloud.*

As my interview progressed, however, and as Dr. Forster boomed forth his knowledge, his recommendations, his desire that I return after having read a rather heaping packet of scientific materials, and after he had quizzed me on where and when I had found so many specimens, particularly of bryozoans, I found a way to raise my voice, to enunciate, to find volume. I did not shout. This was something altogether different. I found a voice that felt steady, true, distinct, one that he could hear through his horn. No more "Speak again!" I found a voice that I had never used before, one that I determined to use again, and not only with Dr. Forster.

Diary Entry

My inevitable trip to the bank was again fraught with disapproval—glares from Banker Whitaker each time I enter his door. My money is safer with him, however, than it would be in my home, and he does help me manage with details, his potential for profit overcoming his evident distaste in having to work with a woman of my reputation—someone "trying to be a man," "trying to be a scientist," "leaving behind the boundaries most women oblige themselves to." I've heard all these things said about me, and yet I continue to read, study, learn, and discover.

"You do not need to take that tone with me," said Whitaker when I asked for more than my usual withdrawal. I hadn't realized I was taking a "tone," only that I was speaking directly. Distinctly.

Is it possible that my sessions with Forster are shaping me toward a clarity that might well disturb the men around me, used as they are to the mildness of women? They want us soft. Tender. Caring. And I forcefully ask for withdrawals that I might purchase books. What is to become of "woman" when I act as I do?

Nell, you must remember to demure yourself!

Diary Entry

My final meeting with Dr. Forster. My readings under his tutelage have been exhaustive, and I have feared each time he interviewed me that I would reveal such ignorance that he would dismiss me with a magisterial wave of his large hand. Even through his thick beard I often saw his mouth curl to a tolerant and bemused smile. His time in Lawrence is soon to end, and instead of his usual questioning he set about thinking toward the future, remarking that Kansas was as good a place for the discovery and study of fossils as anywhere he had been. The discoveries in the western part of the state promised greater finds in the future. My own work with bryozoans he deemed necessary to future understanding. He applauded my careful logging, as I now note all that Samuel has taught me to include. I read a section map with some alacrity. Dr. Forster wonders if the exact time of the discovery is necessary to the record. Nevertheless, I persist. As Samuel has said, why not include rather than exclude information readily available to me?

Dr. Forster admonished me on one point. "These discoveries you make, how long do you examine the same area, and how often do you return to find more?" In two instances he had noticed that the types of bryozoans I'd found did not seem entirely compatible with what one might expect of the fossil record. Was I perhaps conflating two sites in my record keeping? How close together were the discoveries? Might I log not only time—if I insisted on it—date and location, but also more carefully the proximity of each fossil in a place to another? This might someday be of great importance. "We assume," he said, "that the fossils we find in the same place, at the same time, all come from the same place and time. But do we know this as fact?"

Think, he cajoled me, telling me I must think like a scientist of the future, for, he speculated, great hypotheses, great revelations, will come from a storehouse of facts, some of which we may not now be thinking to record. "What of the weather?" he asked. "A fossil found in late December might well have been discovered on a cold day, but is that so? Did the temperature dip below the freezing point the night before? Or did it snow, or rain, or hail?" He wants to know the conditions of the present discovery in great detail. "And what vegetation grew at the site?" he asked. "Someday we might search for fossils based on the vegetation that now grows from the soil made from the rocks in which we find those fossils."

Perhaps this time my smile was bemused, for he intensified his assertions. "We are not just collecting fossils," he spluttered, "we are collecting data, and we will be long dead and turned to dust before we know what we have found, for the earth is more rich and complicated than we will ever know. Each time we write down a fact we contribute to that complexity, for the scientist's job is not merely to explain, but to question, to enrich, to complicate. Be someone who complicates our simple assertions. In the future, no matter how hard we have worked, and no matter what we manage to assert as true, our conclusions will seem as quaint as Lucretius's explanation of lightning."

With such admonitions, and with resolve to heed Dr. Forster's call, I bid goodbye, my head swimming. I had read Lucretius, or tried to, and his science did seem quaint. That mine would always be equally quaint was disconcerting and reassuring at the same time.

Letter to Sister Mary

Dearest Mary—

I am about to set out upon adventure. I shall accompany my acquaintance Hugh Cameron on his quadrennial pilgrimage to Washington, DC, to attend the inaugural of our new president, General Ulysses S. Grant, March 4 of next year. Cameron has promised a meeting with Grant, through his extensive political connections, though I wonder at the security of his reputation there, for that same reputation suffers year by year here in Kansas as Mr. Cameron's eccentricities seem to grow as profusely as his flowing beard.

He claims the trip can be made in a little over two months' time, and proposes to leave Lawrence just after the New Year. "Should the weather besiege us, or should we lag, then, and only then, will we rely on other conveyances than our feet," he said. Foot is fine with me, for what I do best I do slowly, and though I shall not be able to collect any fossil specimens should I find them, I can make note of where they are, for myself or for future hunters.

I will write more to you soon.

Your loving sister, Nell

Diary Entry

He is a seasoned walker, deliberate, his stride outdistancing mine. I am a mouse scurrying after a horse. Of course, I am distracted by scrutiny. His eyes fairly gleam, as though they could draw him to the horizon. Mine are forever fixed on the roadway, the bluffs when they appear, the creeks, gulches, ravines, and draws. Anywhere water washes the earth, I tarry.

Hugh sits for ten minutes of each hour. He gathers his great ticking watch from his pocket, releases the face cover, finds a log, or a large stone, or the inviting grass, and rests. "Even God rested on the seventh day," he says.

He taunts me often, knowing, as he does, that the Biblical creation story in Genesis is but mythology for me. "Finely wrought debris," he calls my fossil finds. On this trip, of course, I cannot pick up what I find. Tempted as I am, I simply imagine the weight of any object, growing as it always does on a long walk. So I am simply exploring. Perhaps I will return should something noteworthy reveal itself to me.

Diary Entry

I have trusted Mr. Cameron the way, for I can think of no more hardy wayfarer. Still, central Missouri is new to me, and were I by myself I would count myself lost. Whenever I see what I consider a landmark—a large rock bluff, a stand of magnificent willows weeping into a marsh, a distinctive home, a mill, a distant set of buildings—I hold it in my memory, retaining its shape and position as I approach, then turning to capture its other shape as I recede from it.

On this cold day, nearly a fortnight into our journey, moisture billowing the air with each morning breath, I felt a rare loneliness seep into my heart. Hugh remained silent, no political ranting, no stories of early Kansas, no lectures contradicting Emerson, no jovial remarks about the false bards Longfellow and Whittier and Holmes, no quoting of scripture, Shakespeare, Whitman, or Burns.

We always make our way around, rather than through, the towns we pass, for, as Hugh says, "We'll not encounter anyone but Missourians for company." So, at day's end, when I prayed that each step be the last, when Hugh approached a large frame home from behind and went to the back door, banging on it and calling his name, I did not know whether to count him insane or my savior.

Savior, I can report, after a warm hearth, tea, beef stew, biscuits, beets, conversation, and claret—though not for Hugh Cameron, for he shuns alcohol in any form. With a Mr. Horace Miller, a free thinker like Hugh, and his wife Sally, a woman well schooled in the charm it takes to dull the wielded sword of sharp opinion at the supper table. She took genuine interest in my scientific quests, as so many intelligent women do. I write this not to pose, puffed with proud feathers, but because I am proud of my sex, who are no longer content to be demure, to curtsy, to accept without question the opinion and rule of conventions.

Sally Miller collects butterflies. Her excursions take her so far afield she must hire a young neighbor, a boy near manhood, to accompany her. She is a large woman, sitting plumply in a capacious chair, and yet her descriptions of monarch, southern cloudywing, fiery skipper, and sachem, and her accounts of their captures, flutter from her mouth fancifully, like the creatures she seeks to understand.

We soon left the men and retired upstairs to view her cases of pinned specimens, each box a different family. Their very names—Hesperiidae, Hylephila, Thorybes, Danaus—sang to me, as do the names of my fossils. Then I had the rare treat of a warm bath and the bed in which I write. I may never leave it.

Diary Entry

A rare treat of a day. My wish of last night nearly came true. Sally brought me tea, and well-buttered toast. She entreated me to rest, for she had taken the liberty of laundering my clothing, and all was still on the line. Hugh, she reported, was off on some sort of errand with Horace, and so we had the day.

After a small dinner, she said, we would take a brief walk to her favorite meditation, which, she explained, was her name for a place that both removed her from herself and at the same time helped her to be herself. "Do you have meditations yourself?" she asked me. And I surprised myself in my answer: "Anywhere I can see the evidence of fossil life, the rich signs of the life before our human lives, those places would be my 'meditations.' Why, the world itself is my meditation!"

When we ate, and dressed, and walked to a small falls to take our seats on a log among sycamore and oak under a clear and windless sky, the January sun almost a silver fire, I knew with rare suddenness all Sally was saying to me. My high-flung rejoinder had been silly. A meditation is a meditation. We women, so much of the time, are alone. Because of station, because our opinions and knowledge are not taken seriously, because we often work alone—yes, we are beset by babies, and have children to instruct. But we are often working with no other women surrounding us, and so our thoughts, at least, are alone. To be truly alone, and not just feeling alone, and embracing that, and nurturing that—that was what Sally meant by meditation. I write this, all from Sally Miller's sighs, and her quiet remark—"Here, am I unpinned."

The men entered the house with clomping boots, hungry for the dinner Sally had allowed me to help her prepare. A chicken, boiled with onion, carrot, potato, and turnip. The restful day increased rather than diminished my appetite, and I held my own at the table with my dining companions, in appetite if not verbiage.

Evidently Hugh had made a speech in regard to his support of the Kansas Impartial Suffrage Association, which in 1867 put to vote the equal suffrage of women and former slaves. Though that amendment failed in Kansas, Hugh is loath to give up the cause, and he had held forth with his usual admixture of the impromptu and lengthy. He had, of course, poked his stick in the fire of old divisions between Missouri and Kansas. He had preached not only the virtues of women as political beings but also as crusaders against the evils of drink. From there, he touched upon all the moral lapses drink might cause, first slavery, then border ruffians, then primitive religion, then a disdain for education—especially for the fairer sex. How could anyone, he surmised, find a place more restrictive than Missouri, nay, the entire South, to all the important rights of man?

We heard the same sermon he had delivered earlier that day, and, I suspect, like Sally Miller, I retreated to the meditation we'd shared earlier. Again, comfortable in bed, the thought crosses my mind to turn back to Lawrence, to end my adventure, which is more Hugh's adventure than it is mine.

Letter to Sister Mary

Dear Mary—

You will see by the postmark on this letter that I am most happily home for the remainder of the winter. I ended my journey with Hugh Cameron upon his encouragement, or should I say at his behest, or the behest of his behavior. Let me explain, for I must tell someone, and who better than you, my confidante?

I could sense Hugh Cameron's agitation in the two days leading up to his break with me. We had a most pleasant visit with his friends in Missouri, Horace and Sally Miller, though the visit ended with the report of Hugh Cameron lecturing an entire town and, by proxy, the state of Missouri and the American South.

When we set out again, he was silent. His pace became inconsistent, waning before he fairly whipped himself forward. Still, he easily outdistanced me. I must have seemed to him to disappear, then reappear, as occasionally he would stop, turn, hands on hips, and shake his head as though bewildered that I was still with him. He would allow me to catch up to him, then he would march forward as though indignant at the wait.

None of Hugh's behavior should have surprised me, eccentric as he is known to be. Had I really supposed that our acquaintanceship would escape the vicissitudes of his character? That the grudges he held would not eventually include me? That his past, so put aside, would not, as it does to us all, leap on his back and make any journey burdensome?

My dear Mary, I have come to believe that he thought me to be his one-time love Priscilla, or at least to represent the shadow that had fallen over his life because of her, for my following him became a source of great unsettlement to him. As we progressed nearer—I realize now—to the place she called home during their courtship, he began muttering—in dialogue with either himself, or with the long-lost Priscilla, but certainly not with me. I could hear only snatches of his outbursts: "Fickle!" "What did you know of me?" "To walk is to settle!" "A ribbon is a binding!" "The road, though a ribbon, is unbound." "I am bound to my beloved Washington." "I am bound to pass by. To be passed by. To pass each day. To pass." Such words, such phrases. A mind revealed by his loose lips, and a distraught mind at that.

"Why are you walking with me?" he said to me finally, his hands on hips once more, his tone scolding. "You think you can find my heart, know my heart, as you know my letters?" And he produced them, still bound by ribbons, from his deep coat pocket. "You cannot!" he exclaimed. "No one may!" He raised the packet of letters skyward.

"I am accompanying you to the inauguration of President Grant," I reminded him. "Nothing more. An adventure through territory previously unknown to me." I spoke slowly, gently, as I used to when I calmed our dog—you may remember the raucous Millicent, ever excitable at the least provocation? She died when you were still young. "General Cameron, I have seen much, have much to return to when time permits, have met your friends, have found myself more sturdy than I supposed."

He seemed calmed by my words, though he still held the packet of letters over his head, as though waiting for them to fly away. When they did not, he slowly returned them to his capacious coat. "I must be by myself," he said. "I must journey alone for a time."

"You have not forgiven me for finding your letters," I said. "You have not forgiven your Priscilla for knowing your heart. I never went searching for your heart, Hugh Cameron, and yet you showed it to me. I am sorry for what I see." And with that I turned from him. I walked west. He did not speak again. He did not follow.

I did not relish being an unaccompanied woman in a strange place, Mary. It is one thing to fossil hunt in and around Lawrence by myself—I seem as eccentric and scandalous to people there as Hugh Cameron. Hugh's journey had shown me an isolated way, his paths always obscure. I knew I could find my way to Sally Miller. I did, and there I was pressed immediately to her bosom, was well-fed and bedded. "Agitation is his way," Horace Miller said over dinner. "It is his virtue, and his vice." I spent a lovely day with Sally Miller. She has taken as passionate an interest in lepidoptera as I have in fossil bryozoans. Her specimens, pinned, wings fanned, in their cases, look all the world like the fanning lace of a colony of Pennsylvanian Septopora. Her butterflies have the softest wings, my fossils the full grit of stone deposit, yet both are lovely and unique, even mysterious, in their design.[*]

Forgive my divergence from the path. I returned home accompanied much of the way by the young man Sally takes with her on her lepidopteran adventures. Though he was not pleased, he also carried a large satchel, which I managed to nearly fill with fossil finds, especially from Jackson County in nearby Kansas City. Once there I packed the satchel under the seat of a train car, and was soon at the depot in Lawrence. As for Hugh Cameron, he may well make the entire journey to Washington, unaccompanied by me, carrying nothing but his sad letters. I hope all will be forgiven upon his return, but in this instance I prefer the solidity of my fossils to the flightiness of Hugh Cameron.

Please come for a visit so that we might speak more intimately of all that has occurred these last months.

I am yours. I send my love, Nell

[*] See figure included here.

in lepidoptery, as I have in ~~fossil~~ bryozoans. Her specimens, pinned, wings fanned, in their cases, look all the world like the fanning lace of a colony of Pennsylvanian Septopora. Her butterflies have the softest wings, my fossils the full grit of stone deposit, yet both are lovely and unique, even ~~myself~~ my strivous, in their design. I will try to trace them here for you, from my diary of that day.

Danaus Vulgaris

Fossil Rock

Letter to Samuel Winston

Saturday, May 1, 1869
Lawrence, KS

Dear Samuel:

I am untoward, a woman past her prime as a woman, widowed these six
years, childless, with no family in Kansas, where I have nothing but a house,
my few friends, a church I have all but abandoned, and my duties to the
community. These were not enough to sustain me, and, as you know, I bent
myself to the study of fossils. Those in my ever-narrowing circle looked at
this pursuit askance, not able to juxtapose the words "woman" and "study"
together. They have been whispering—I have heard it in their very demean-
ors, if that is possible—for several years about me. Now they whisper and
gossip about my relationship with you, the one who has supported my
interest in fossil creatures. Reputation, repute—what horrible words.

For, as we both know, what they say is not wholly true, though it might
well have been but for my reluctance, my sudden tears where there might
have been sudden joy. I have always come to you for study, for enlightenment, for your judgement and interest in the fledgling science outlined by
Darwin. I have come to you as student. I accompany you, and you accompany me, not on desultory liaisons on sandbars or at the bluffs above the
river, but on scientific excursions. I, in your presence, and you, in mine,
have made what you have called "discoveries of import," and I know this
to be true. Your enthusiasms have infected mine, as mine have yours. Is
enthusiasm, especially in a woman, so suspect?

Yet even as others suspect me, I suspect myself. My discoveries include
you. My glance, oft bent toward the ground, sometimes rises to find your

pleasant face, your lips pursed with whatever your lively mind contains. I study you as I study the texts you've given me to peruse. My heart opens, as does my mind. What others say is not true—not yet. But I am emboldened by this past week spent hunting for fossil specimens. Having already lost my reputation, what is lost in making speculation become truth? I have trained my eye to the smallest of creatures as found in rock. I have trained my eye to your smallest gestures, expressions, inflections of voice. I think I have made a discovery. Of our shared feelings. Yes, you are a man in your prime. Yes, you are the educated and accomplished. Yes, you have the respect of your colleagues that has built your reputation as a geologist.

I have none of those things, nothing but a sullied reputation. Whispers usually follow deeds. I have no deeds, only whispers. We must speak aloud together of this matter, and decide what future to bring to fruition.

Sincerely, Nell Doerr

Diary Entry

The note was delivered by a towheaded boy I had never seen before. He stood in the doorway, hand outstretched, but with the envelope folded backward, as though he were hiding it. "From the professor," he said. He did not move forward, and I knew he expected a tip. I clucked my tongue, and retreated inside for a one-cent piece. Tip granted, he nearly threw the note at me and bolted to the street. I stood in the open doorway and read Samuel's scrawled message: "Meet me at the river! At dusk!"

Jane flew past my head before I remembered I'd let her from her cage for a few moments of freedom. The fluttering blue of her wings took her to the cherry tree, the fruit just ripening, and she bent her beak to that new reddening. My throat caught. How would I coax her back to her cage when the spring air was so crisp, the sky blue as her feathers, the fruit in such abundance? I called to her, whistled, warbled. I held out my finger, to which she always flew when indoors, tucking her beak meekly beneath a wing. She was deaf to calls, to gestures. She was frantic in the cherries. She would be sick, I thought. Sick with the excess that came from indulgence. She was an Eve who would gain no knowledge. The sun lengthened the shadows, bringing a slight chill. I folded the note and went inside for my shawl. I left the door open; Jane would return to her cage after she had tasted enough of fruit and freedom. Sometimes, small tastes of these things are enough to satisfy her.

Note Found in Diary

[No date]

Nell, you must take hold of yourself. What you have done without shame should remain shameless. When you pass the church, why do you speed your pace? When in the mercantile, you ask for what you want, you pay for it and leave, yet your eyes do not meet Henderson's. Isn't your purchase all he should attend to, rather than his attention to the business of what might be said of your personal life? That thread of privacy, once so easy to knot toward decency, now blows so freely in the wind of rumor and gossip. What can you grasp?

That you are guilty? A woman of lost reputation, a mannish woman more interested in scientific evidence than spiritual matters, a woman content to be unaccompanied, a woman who will not take her turn as hostess for tea, who will not provide refreshment for evening worship, who might be absent from her home for days without disclosing her whereabouts, a woman once a substantial member of a substantial company of founders of the city, now foundering, lost, in the halls of the university, on the bluffs above the river, on the sandbars where you have been seen to enter a tent with Samuel.

What can you grasp? That you are loved. You are respected. You are learning what few can comprehend. That you have chosen to live, to truly live, when your life might have been buried in duty, in acceptance, in convention. You will not live out your life in a way expected of women. You will become not woman, not female, but creature, like the very creatures you study and come to understand. Perhaps in so doing, you will understand yourself.

Nell, take hold of yourself.

Letter from Hugh Cameron

Thursday, June 10, 1869
Cameron's Bluff

Dear Nell Doerr:

As you can see, I have enclosed several fossil specimens found on my trek home from the inaugural festivities. I offer them as apology and in peace.

You missed much ceremony, but you did not miss much in our President Grant, who refused to ride in the same coach as President Johnson. Johnson therefore stayed away, signing legislation, leaving his successor to say what all presidents will say under oath and then repeat as speech: that they will enforce the laws. Our general did make one comment of insight, something to the effect that the best way to rid the nation of a bad law is through its stringent enforcement. We found that out in Kansas, did we not, when federal law was on the wrong side of history?

I invite you to resume your fossil hunting on the bluff at any time you wish, and I will continue to supply you with what I am able to. I remember your counsel from your Dr. Forster, and will try either to describe well, or lead you to my discoveries that you might fulfill his wishes for facts and information. I am well rested from my journey at this point and, as I respect your pursuits, I hope that you can respect mine.

I write in friendship, Hugh Cameron

Diary Entry

It is my birthday, I having reached the doubling of fours. 44, I write, and can hardly believe it. Father Robert has reached the doubling of sixes, 66, and Mother Jo is 60. I live so far from Pine Bluff, Arkansas. Each birthday I want nothing but home. I want to sit by the hearth, those red stones stacked and mortared by my father when I was still a baby in Mother Jo's arms, Hiram and Mary not yet arrived to complete our family. I want Father Robert and Mother Jo young again, as I want myself young again. I want to pour the small glass of whisky for Father Robert, the small stem of sherry for Mother Jo, as I did when I was seven. I want to sit next to them with my cider, lamps burning, as we read, as reading has always been sacred to them both, as they learned while I learned. Learning was celebrated, as it is even more passionately in Kansas. My childhood learning and reading was simpler. A passage from Pilgrim's Progress. *A poem from Robert Burns, about a mouse turned up in a field, its home ruined, its life changed, "the best-laid plans gang aft aglay." And Burns would write about the mouse being luckier than mankind. For the mouse is neither beset by the anxieties of the past nor the fears of the future. At home, growing up, I was the mouse. Now I am the woman, with equal parts regret and fear. "Father," I would say on this birthday, were I sitting next to him, "the world is not as I thought it might be. I have disappointed you." And he would shrug, take a sip of whisky, wrinkle his brow and eyes, and expect me to finish with, "I have not married. I have no children. I live far away. I do what many cannot understand, especially in a woman—I read science and collect specimens that reveal the ancient life of earth."*

"Are you happy?" he would ask. And I would nod, and he would say, "Then I am happy." And I might tell him of a discovery, and my hopes of discovery, and he would say, "You always could find things. Nothing went missing in our house."

And I wouldn't have the heart to say my mind: "Nothing went missing except me."

Letter to Samuel Winston

Samuel—

You are much to me. First, you were my teacher, then my companion, and then . . . more. Though men are often reviled by women, especially those in my situation, I regard you without blame. I wish you to feel no remorse, just as I feel no remorse. Nothing you have done, nor could do, would ever change all that you have given me: your knowledge, your support, your enthusiasm, your sympathies, and your regard for me.

You are a young man. I am a woman beyond my prime, unable to bear children, forty-four years of age. In the world we study, a human lifetime is less than the time a shooting star meets the eye. You have said how little human time, human age, means to you. I agree, and yet I have always been a person who concerned herself deeply with the time in which I live. My abolitionist fervor was once as powerful as my fervor for science and knowledge. I cannot forget the power of those early relationships I forged in K.T. and with the admission of Kansas as a Free State. To a person, I have shocked those friends with my interest in fossils, and, with that, my untoward interest in you.

I know that I sought you. Again, you are without blame. Samuel, our conquests—me of you and you of me—were matters of flesh. Our conquests in the fossil world are so much more substantial, and will remain forever in the annals of the history of paleontology. Stone is more permanent than flesh, as it contains the life of the past, fossilized to be sure, but there for us to study. Anything else we do together is temporary, and I must renege on its importance to me as you must its importance to you.

I have heard through our mutual friend Professor Snow that you might have opportunities in California, where some exciting prospects for academic life and fossil records await you. Fly to them, Samuel. Do not be tied to me, or to our history together. I do not discount that coldly, but warmly. That warmth, however, is in the past, just as I will soon be in your past. I hold you in the highest regard, but I have more regard for what you will accomplish in your future, which is, again, as bright as that shooting star.

Best regards, my dear young man,
Nell Johnson Doerr

.

Sample of Nell's Log, with Drawings

Thursday, September 23, 1869

Archimedes, Permian (?), Pennsylvanian (?), Douglas County, Lawrence
Township, Section 3, on Cameron's bluff, discovered 14:02, September 15,
1869, a cloudless day, among loose erosions.

Rhombopora lepidodendroides, branching and fenestrate, from Douglas County, on Kansas River, north of Lecompton Township, Section 8, discovered between 10:22 and 13:07, September 19, 1869, a cloudy day threatening rain, among other debris on sandbar.

Letter from Dr. Smith, Paleontologist

Monday, January 3, 1870
National Museum, Washington, DC

Dear N. J. Doerr—

This is to acknowledge receipt of your detailed sketches and most thorough logs of your discoveries of bryozoan fossils. Yes, the National Museum would indeed be most interested in adding many of them to our collection. As you may know, we have regular shipments from the western part of your state, where remarkable discoveries are being made. Your invertebrates, however, need study, and some of your discoveries will fill rather large gaps in our collection and in our knowledge of bryozoans.

I have enclosed a shipping address along with a detailed list of which of those fossils that you logged will serve us best at this time. If you will ship them at your expense, we will send money once we know the cost. If that is a burden to you, for you do not write of your circumstances, please investigate costs to ship so that we might send you an advance.

By all means, as you continue to collect, you must send along your drawings and logs, particularly of bryozoan discoveries. We hope that this exchange will be the first of many.

Most Sincerely,
Dr. J. L. Smith
National Museum

Letter to Dr. Smith

Thursday, March 3, 1870
Lawrence, KS

Dear Dr. Smith—

I am N. J. Doerr, Nell Johnson Doerr, the widow of Solomon Doerr, a brave man killed mercilessly by William C. Quantrill nearly seven years ago. Since his death I have dedicated myself to the discovery of fossils, particularly bryozoans of all kinds. In 1863 I was but poorly educated in the sciences, but I sought instruction at the University of Kansas from Professor Francis H. Snow, and I worked with Samuel Winston, now at the University of California, and for a brief time with Dr. Leonard Forster, who was in residence at the university for nearly two months in 1868.

I admit fully to being but an amateur scientist, curious, self-educated, voracious in pursuit of both the fossil record and in the proper way to document that record. Dr. Winston and Dr. Forster admonished me to log thoroughly, and I have tried to follow their advice. I am unsure of my skills in rendering my fossils, and I hope you will not be disappointed when you have them before you. I admit to being somewhat overwhelmed, though quite pleased, by your positive response to my tentative letter to you. I will immediately do your bidding and send to you the specimens you've requested. If you can correspond with me further, and let me know what, if anything, I could learn to do better, or what you are looking for specifically, I will try my best to comply with your wishes.

Although I am a woman, and but an amateur, I do hope to make a contribution. Everywhere I have read that we have much work to do as we document the evolution of the earth, so much work that each and all of us might be able to add to the prehistoric record. As I have no children, and have enough means to meet my daily needs, I intend to make it my work to help in this grand enterprise. Thank you for accepting my wish to make a difference. I will continue to correspond that you might choose those specimens most worthwhile to the National Museum.

Sincerely,
Nell Johnson Doerr

Letter from Sally Miller

May 24, 1870
Waverly, MO

Dear Nell—

I am mightily pleased to receive your letter of April 30. How gratified you must be, to be sending your fossils somewhere so that they will contribute to the national understanding of science. Might I be emboldened to write in a similar way, offering whatever of my humble collection of butterflies, captured from such a small radius of my rural Missouri home, to a national museum? Horace regards such a thought as superfluous, and has told me so more than once. Surely everyone knows about everything that I've managed to net and pin and describe, he says.

I have recently taken to watercolor, so that I might render my sketches in the brilliant colors, the mosaic patterns, the sharp contrasts that butterflies seem to embody so well. Like fluttering flowers, they are. Horace admires them as art—more than science—he says. That fits his sense of what a woman ought to be doing. Painting is, in his mind, more the role of a woman than science. Nell, I have never disobeyed Horace. I took my marriage vows as every woman does, to love, honor, and obey. I have never had difficulty obeying Horace. Perhaps that is because he has never made it difficult. Now, I fear he rather is.

May I confess, Nell? I have already posted a letter to the National Museum, unbeknownst to Horace. Should I have a return post, he will discover it as he picks up the mail at the post office, and demand to know the contents. Should the answer be as he thinks it would be, that my collection is not unique nor of scientific interest, the pleasure of being right will outweigh the irritation that I wrote a letter he did not think appropriate to my station and sex. Should the answer show an interest in my collection—drawings or specimens—irritation will become anger. I fear he would forbid any attempt I might make to share what I have developed such a passion for. Then whatever will I do?

Am I underestimating Horace? Am I overestimating myself and my work? How do you think your Solomon would have reacted to your interest in fossils, had his life not been cut short by such violence? I hope that is not a painful speculation to ask you to make. Of course, I do not expect you to solve these mysteries of marriage and ambition. You alone are someone to whom I can write such questions. Though we live far apart, I feel such a closeness to you. We are fellow travelers on roads not always well mapped for us.

Write me of your life. Do not rush to ameliorate my self-doubts, for letters, when sent from a distance, often address but momentary concerns, already resolved or dissipated by the time they are answered.

I send you my love,
Sally Miller

Letter to Sally Miller

Friday, July 31, 1870
Lawrence, KS

Dearest Sally—

I am bereft with your news. Why, so often, do those around us present us with what they call a "choice," and yet there is no choice at all? I cannot, of course, tell you how to choose, for it is odd to think that one might have to choose between a husband and the sharing of a collection of butterflies. You asked me how I thought Solomon might react to my fossils, their collection, the knowledge and study I have to make, my relationships with men of science, my need to assert myself to get money for packaging, and shipping, and so on. I cannot tell you. Once a husband is no longer alive, one tends to think the best of him. What would Solomon say and do in all these circumstances? I remember Solomon with nothing but fondness, with an eye toward believing in his most generous tolerations of my stubbornesses, his loving discourse as I shared ideas, his quick embraces of affection. Memory corrects toward perfection, so I have tended to think the best of how he might react. Probably I am wrong, for if immortality brings courage, mortality brings fear, and we all fear change.

Were I forbidden, as you are, to share my collection and sketches, I believe I would still collect, and still sketch, if for no other reason than that someday, hopefully, I would find leniency and permission. Please tell me you have not stopped what brings you so much solace, even as you accept that you cannot now share with the scientific community. I thought maybe I should ask Dr. Smith to write Horace a letter making a case for the importance of what so many men and women are doing for science. Would

Horace listen to a distinguished man who contacted him directly? We women are mostly amateurs, of course, without the heft of authority, and so we bear the burden of being questioned for our desire to understand and share the interesting, even puzzling, ways of the earth. Why, even Benjamin Mudge, professor at the State Agricultural College, trained himself. He gave up the law to become professional in what had always been his fascination with the outdoors. He was first Kansas State Geologist, and conducted our first geological survey. He has made important discoveries and will continue to do so, I am certain. Already he sends some of his findings to Marsh at Yale and Cope in Philadelphia.

I fear I am rambling, trying to assert courage into what you must find a difficult position. Do as you are doing, for what else are you equipped to do? For what else in this world will you have a passion? I remember a Bible passage about not hiding our light in a secret place, under a bushel. Have you read it? I hope your Horace will someday see your light for what it is—the brightness of your mind and soul, something to be shared.

Come for a visit if you can, for if I could say these things directly to your ears, holding your hand in mine, you would see how sincere I am in my admiration of you, and how distraught I am by this news.

Most sincerely,
Nell

Diary Entry

Today is the seventh anniversary of the raid. Last night I lay in bed in equal parts saddened and cheered. I was saddened by memory and loss, cheered by the prospect of discovery. One of our shuddering thunderstorms grumbled across Lawrence, shafts of lightning stunning the earth, no doubt shattering trees. Thunder rattled the windows of my house. Rain swarmed the sky, pummeled the roof, gushed into guttering. For an hour or more wind rushed through the cracks in the wall, soughing and moaning. I waited through the long night, all the while mourning the loss of Solomon and anticipating the morning.

Weather is a boon companion for a fossil hunter. Thunderstorms do not create fossils, but they create fossil discoveries. Erosion is a sculptor that wears away rock to reveal the beauty of a prismopora *or a* thamniscus *or a* leioclema. *On the same path, the familiar bluff, the dry sandbar now sifted by water, treasures are exposed in the humid sunlight that follows our fiercest storms.*

That such violence could reveal such beauty. The human violence of thundering hooves and gunshot and cannon brings nothing but misery and despair. The violence of nature renews, reveals, reasserts life. How I love weather in all its forms. Cold and ice to crack. Wind and water to erode. Heat and drought to fissure the earth. A great shifting tide it is, much like the tides of the ancient sea in this place long ago, before humans and our tendencies toward discord and violence.

Lightning—strike! Thunder—roar! Rain—deluge! Wind—whip! I celebrate you above and beyond the drunken bevy of Quantrill—those strikes, whips, and roars of raiders so bent on destruction rather than discovery.

Letter to Dr. Smith

Thursday, September 15, 1870
Lawrence, KS

Dear Dr. Smith:

You have asked after what you call my "prowess" in the discovery of fossils. To answer properly, I must admit that I have always been adept at finding things. Here's how. You don't look for objects. You create the conditions in which what is lost might find you. Let's say your father has lost his pocket watch, the thin fob finally fraying and letting the watch tumble anywhere.

Do you immediately run to the field where your father was cutting hay? Do you run to the barn where he harnessed and unharnessed the bay team? Do you send brother and sister throughout the house, retracing your father's daily pacings from bed to table to sitting room to porch to outhouse to wash basin? No, you do not, for you are looking for a pocket watch, and not for your father. Think of the watch. Think of its weight. Think of the thinly braided fob your mother wove to harness the watch to your father. Think of when the watch might have been consulted, for any other time it would have been securely pocketed. Talk to your father. Did he consult his watch? When? At what moment did he realize it had gone missing? Let him tell you the story of the watch, a deathbed gift from his father, not of great value, often giving the wrong time, but a valued possession nevertheless. And ask your mother about the fob, woven when, and why? Because your father always worried he might lose it, yet still insisted on carrying it each day. Examine the frayed fob, the extended fibers left when the remainder tore away. At least three inches of it might still be attached to the watch. You see it swinging, like the pendulum of a clock. You walk to the stable where at least twice you have scraped your knuckles on the protruding nail on the stall door. The watch hangs from that nail, waiting for you.

Dr. Smith, fossils wait for me, especially after flood and rain. They love erosion—wind and water. You don't seek them, Sir. They wait, eager for discovery, and reveal themselves. Like plants, they have their seasons—fall and spring for the weather, winter for the snow melt, the rocks frozen and cracking and crumbling, summer to bake the outlines of creatures to their whiteness against the tan stone. You do not need to look, you simply need to see.

Sincerely,
Nell Johnson Doerr

Letter to Sister Mary

Monday, November 28, 1870
Lawrence, KS

My dear Mary—

I have returned safely to Lawrence, though I have left a great deal behind me in Pine Bluff. When I climbed down the steps onto the train platform, I wondered if it was solid ground. Everything there in Pine Bluff—my first home, my first family, especially you, Michael, Sara and John—seemed weighty, and as substantial as earth. Here, for the first two days, I felt adrift.

Perhaps I am remembering my first journey here, with all that I left tugging back at me—my Benjamin, my Lawrence, your Sara and John, then only eight and six years old and the apples of my eye. I was down to the core then, when I first came to K.T.—no sweet fruit left to sustain me.

Now I am sustained by my recent visit, by what will always be cherished memory. Sara made a lovely bride, as she will make a lovely wife. After her loss of Herman, she might never have recovered life and heart, especially after that poor soldier survived battle, capture, escape, bullet, and amputation, only to be jostled off the train platform in a moment of merriment and celebration. With no arm to catch himself, with no arms to hold him. To live through so much, only to die. The war took so many Hermans in just such an arbitrary fashion.

I know what it is, such loss. We women become soldiers, too, marching forward just as Sara did, in spite of wound, amputation, the imprisonment by grief, which locks us into a cell to which only we have the key. Sara turned that key, and last week stepped into radiance—her face, her happy young man, her sureness of voice in saying, "I do." You are lucky. She is lucky. I am lucky, and not only because of circumstance, but because of what we have made of circumstance. Dearest sister, no wonder I miss you.

The double pleasure of a double wedding. More luck, more happy circumstance, that John should find such a bride. I know that the coincidence of courtships was simply accident, but I cannot thank your family enough for the thoughtful twinned ceremonies. Two brides. Two grooms. Four young people who will be our future. John's Olivia will make a fine minister's wife once he finishes his education at Oberlin and finds a congregation. His faith—in his life, in his new wife, in his God—seems a beacon. A minister is nothing if not an example, and I cannot think of a better man to emulate.

Mary, I revel in the two weeks I've had with you, for you, too, are someone to emulate. Your truest sympathies, your generous heart, your wise counsel. I will mind all we said as I move forward in my life here in Lawrence. I vow to visit you more often, for you and Michael and now Sara and Walter, and John and Olivia, have made me more whole again. I may feel afloat, adrift, insubstantial, as I place feet again in my life here, but this visit, and your words, have grounded me toward a new rootedness in all I do.

Write to me soon.

Your loving sister,
Nell

P.S. My parrot Jane died while I was away. Winnie Terrant was so afraid the fault was hers, for I had taken the cage and bird to her for care. Jane had been sick several times, losing feathers, her eyes weeping. My only regret was that Winnie buried Jane. I would have taken her to the university and had her stuffed to add to their growing collection. I did not say that to Winnie, though, for she would have thought me morbid, and the best she could offer me was, "We prayed properly for her soul."

Note to Jacob Whitaker

Friday, March 31, 1871

To: Jacob Whitaker, President, First National Bank, Lawrence

You have refused the draft on my account for the shipment of three crates on the Union Pacific railroad, or so I was informed today when I arrived at the station with one more crate. The station master reports that he was informed by First National Bank Vice President J. B. Watson that my account lacked sufficient funds to cover the cost of my shipment. This is nonsense. Mr. Watson should be disciplined for violating the charter of your bank, for his small-minded prejudice against my scientific work, and for embarrassing me without cause. I expect word by return post that you have rectified this situation entirely, and within the next two days.

Sincerely,
Nell Johnson Doerr

Diary Entry

Mr. Jenkins knocked loudly on the door at an hour when I am used to quiet. "If you want your shipment on today's train, you must have everything in order by ten o'clock. Not a moment more." And so there went deliberation and care. I hurriedly climbed to my specimens room. The odor I'd noticed the night before seemed stronger, creating a noxious atmosphere, and I was no closer to its cause. I tied a kerchief over my nose, that I might breathe only from my mouth, but still the odor penetrated cloth as assuredly as it had begun to drift down the stairs. Rather than avoid the smell, I chose confrontation. I tore kerchief from face and bent to the floor. I traversed the length of the wall that faced outside. I turned and sniffed along the outer wall, my view of the side yard and its flowers making me wish I were smelling them instead. Then along the chimney wall. The chimney. Yes, and the small crevice where plaster did not quite meet bricks, but where smell met nose.

Distractions. No doubt this dying creature, be it mouse, rat, squirrel, or possum, was not thinking about my work. I would box specimens, fewer than anticipated, then purchase lye from Woodward & Finely. Properly placed, that should help reduce the smell, replacing it with dry bone, trapped in wall, powerless to interrupt my work again.

Would that all cures to such ills be so easy.

Note to Hugh Cameron

Dear Hugh—

As you have continued to believe in my scientific pursuits, and because of the urgency I feel in delivering my most recent discoveries to Washington, DC, may I humbly beseech you to meet me at your earliest convenience at the Union Pacific Depot with ten dollars so that crates impeded by Wood-house (I would prefer he be named Wood<u>shack</u>, given his shoddiness in preventing me yet again from drawing from my bank draft) might find their home among other such exciting discoveries in our Nation's Capital?

I am, as always, indebted to you for your aid.

Sincerely, Nell

Diary Entry

*My anger boils and boils, though to no end. The men I can only think of as ene-
mies incite me as though for sport. The Reverend Littlefield chastises me that I am
not in church. Banker Whitaker refuses me access to my money, duly deposited,
with receipt, by the National Museum. Railroad agents Jenkins and Woodhouse
listen to the minister and banker. My champion Hugh Cameron, with his many
eccentricities, sometimes rather hurts than helps my endeavors in Lawrence.*

*Anger turns to frustration and then to evisceration. That is what this commu-
nity wants, their brains and vision for the future as small as the brains and
future of the dinosaurs, those same creatures whose bones they refuse to acknowledge, much less study.*

*Nell, you must be civil. You will remain civil. Bury your anger just as your
dear fossils are buried—you know where both can be found. Look to the day when
you might use them to your ends. Remember, nothing frustrates a man more than
a strong woman, and, better, a strong woman who remains calm.*

Letter to Dr. Smith

Dear Dr. Smith:

I am in receipt of your kind letter of September 24, clarifying my relationship to the National Museum. The title of Field Representative seems fitting, as my fieldwork consumes a great deal of my time. I only *hope* to wear the mantle of "representative." This for two reasons. The first, I humbly admit, is that I do not feel worthy to represent such an important institution, given my education, training, and knowledge. Yet I aspire to gain purchase in each of these areas, and someday be fit for you.

Secondly, however, "representative" is a *hopeful* title to give a woman unattached to a man, because it assumes position, authority, and rank. In Lawrence, Kansas, women do not easily win respect enough to gain any of the latter. My position is misunderstood, my authority is nil, and my rank is defined only in terms of my sex.

Dr. Smith, you may write to me such compliments and give me such titles as you wish. I still struggle to bank the drafts on your account which you so generously send. I am still harassed by stationmasters and railroad agents. I am still questioned as though I am a child. People here misunderstand me, and science, and my fossils, and your collection and its importance. I will continue in my work. I will remain your field representative. Might you print a small card with my name and relationship to the museum, that I might have something more than my anger to show those of slow wit here in Kansas?

Thank you for considering this request.

I am yours sincerely,
Nell Johnson

Letter to Mother Jo

Friday, June 7, 1872
Lawrence, KS

Dear Mother Jo:

Do not be alarmed at the hand that writes this letter. I must dictate, and Margaret Littlefield is kindly here to help. She gives you her greetings, and I force her to write what a generous soul she has been the last two days. I cannot write. I cannot grasp a teacup, never mind the bucket, pan, plate, or utensil. I am a baby, helpless, and must be fed.

Margaret insists I tell you of my circumstances, and the purpose of this letter, so that she can post it this afternoon. The story is simple. I overreached. I stood on a bluff above the river, and below me, on a shelf of rock, I saw two perfect specimens, lacy, fairly sparkling in their whiteness, lying unattached, waiting for me. I lay down and leaned toward them, to no avail. I inched forward, past my bosom to my pelvis—yes, I am insisting Margaret write those words, though they mortify her. They are scientific enough. You can guess that in my greed to lift those fossils from the shelf, I pitched forward. My right arm is broken, and my left wrist. They were supposed to break my fall, and not themselves crumple and break. The doctor has set them and splinted them toward healing. I may not strain them in any way for two or three weeks. I am to be housebound, as well, when I want to be out searching. You see, when I fell, I lost Solomon's pocket watch, which is ever my companion, as he was, lost though he has been for nearly nine years. Besides noting place, I must record the exact time that I make my discoveries. I must find that watch.

In the meantime, Reverend Littlefield has organized a very brigade of Unitarian women to bring meals, another command to see to my morning dressing and evening preparation for bed. I do not yet sleep well because of the pain.

Hence the purpose of this letter. Though Margaret and the others insist on the lightness of such duty, I need you, Mother Jo. They insist I am not straining their generosity and good will, but I am. I say this in part—and Margaret is loath to write it down, though she must—because for some time I have strained my relationship with them, and the church, with my fossil hunting, my science, and my lack of attendance to church affairs. All is easily understood and forgiven, Margaret insists, and you do not need to hurry to my side, she is telling me. Please come, if you can spare the time. I miss you, and now is a time that brings together physical and filial need.

I dare say that these women now at my side would enjoy visiting with you again—Margaret agrees—for they enjoyed the pleasure of your company upon the occasion of your last visit.

Come to me if you are able. I am strong and will heal quickly. My swelling has shrunken considerably, and once the intense pain subsides, and I eat with more appetite, I will gain strength. As you know, I have a watch and then fossils to find.

I have church affairs to attend to as well, Margaret reminds me. I must end by sending you my love. Margaret is ready to fold paper into envelope and rush to the post office.

Your daughter, Nell

Diary Entry

Reverend Littlefield, as Margaret had suggested he might, came to call. I was ready for my nap, but I served him tepid tea, for I'd made a usual pot earlier. Two o'clock finds me indoors, as hot as Kansas becomes, and my eyes tired after morning reading and the three or so hours of fossil hunting.

Margaret had told him of my desire to return to Sunday worship. "A most positive step," he called it. "For one can and must reconcile God and Nature, just as one does mind and body."

"I acknowledge few such dichotomies," I said, "or rather I have grown tired of them. Women's spheres, men's spheres. Spiritual matters, material matters. The idealistic and the practical."

"As you have so well demonstrated these past years," he said.

I held up my hand to interrupt whatever he might say next, but to no effect. "Mrs. Littlefield, however, suggested you might want to discuss with me your return to services."

"Your Margaret has been a true friend," I said.

"As I might be." He sipped at his tea then, his eyes drifting to my dining table, covered with recent specimens. I confessed that I had lived rather alone for some time. That if I was tired of dichotomies I was also tired of maintaining them by myself. That in my scientific study and work I saw nothing—as was also true of Charles Darwin—that shrunk my astonishment and wonder at creation. In fact my view of creation seems to rely on miracles as much as Genesis *did.*

"Is coincidence, is chance, to be confused with miracle?" he challenged me. Other theologians questioned natural selection and the development of the complex from the simple with the same arguments. Littlefield actually believes much of what Darwin wrote, as it turns out. He has surmounted the obstacle of time, of the

seven-day creation, of the earth's age, of the literal language of so much of the Bible.

"But the essential mystery, the initial spark, the first inkling of life. How to explain that with science? Why not believe in some kind of creator? Some kind of divinity? Some kind of instigator that set matter into motion?"

Like so many, including my own weak and hesitant self, he could believe greatly in the logic and beauty of science as long as it did not distract him from the most fundamental belief—in God.

"Like you," I said, "I have a weakness for the ease, for the comfort, of belief."

"Quite the contrary," he said, putting his teacup on the table beside my fossils. He insisted that belief was not, in fact, comforting or safe. Belief and faith meant leaps of courage. They demanded the same challenges that scientists struggle with as they question. "Belief," he clarified, "is a kind of inquiry into the relationship with the unseen, the unknown, the unknowable, in fact. Might that not take even more daring than science, which comes only to prove the knowable?"

"Might we have the courage for both?" I asked, rather enjoying his thoughtfulness and energy.

"I will see you at worship on Sunday," he said, and rose from his chair. He smiled. "Thank you for this discussion."

I led him to the door.

We are Unitarian, I thought. We strive to unify, to bring together religions and philosophies. And now, science.

Letter to Sally Miller

Tuesday, September 3, 1872
Lawrence, KS

Dear Sally—

In the bustle of our daily lives, we too often forget those we love and cherish, hoping for news, but not often enough seeking it. I seek it now, for you have been silent. Perhaps, as you wrote before, you feel silenced by the tight grip of Horace's admonition that you not share your work, your love, of lepidoptera. Perhaps, as I encouraged you toward disobedience, you cannot bear writing about a life of obedience, if that is what you have chosen, fearing I would disapprove of you. That was not my intention, certainly, for our friendship is not based on your obedience to my advice, nor to the requirements of your marriage. Instead, we are kindred spirits, no matter what decisions we make. Internally, we are sisters, and I miss you, my sister.

Might you be able to come for a visit, or perhaps welcome one from me? Here you will find that I was finally able to rebuild the porch Solomon so lovingly built me so many years ago. How pleasant to sit outside on a cool evening. As for me, you will find changes, too, at least in demeanor. After a nasty fall that broke my right arm and my left wrist, I was so well taken care of—first by the women of my Unitarian Church, whom I had supposed to have abandoned me, and then by my dear Mother Jo—that I decided to turn toward gratitude. And perhaps that is why I write to you, now that I am sufficiently recovered to host or travel, and want to see those who mean much to me. If science requires that we connect discovery with observation with fact, then friendship surely requires the same.

You do not have to answer my questions nor pay attention to my advice about your science, but I would like to hear how you are doing, as I rely on the knowledge of our friendship, even when we cannot visit each other often enough. I must say I thought of you during my days recovering from my fall. These were days when I was not able even to turn the pages of a book without discomfort, and I certainly could not pursue my passion for fossils—for being out of doors, eyes searching, hoping always to discover. I know that is how you felt about your butterflies, that openness to whatever you might see, because at some point you will see what you have never seen before. The Kansas Academy of Sciences has just begun to publish papers delivered during their annual meetings. The listing of butterflies is staggering to me, as one unfamiliar with such variety in what I study. The Latin and common names—

> *Dione vanilae*—Red Silverspot
> *Euptoieta Claudia*—Dull Meadow
> *Grapta interrogationis*—The Question Mark
> *Thecla cerops*—Hubner's Hairstreak
> *Cataopsilia eubule*—The Cloudless Yellow
> *Hesperia montivago*—Checkered Skipper

What wonders these must be to behold, I can only imagine. I hope even if you are no longer collecting, you are at least as open to discovery and science as you always have been.

Please write soon to let me know of your condition, of your life. Remember that you should share all with me, as my heart is open to you. Thank you for your friendship.

Yours truly,
Nell

Diary Entry

In my walk today I stumbled upon the creature Caleb. Everyone calls him "Caliban," for he seems more animal, with his stooped walk and his sudden gestures, than human. He is but ten years old, born just after the raid. Some say he was scarred in the womb by his mother's trauma and grief. He is not known to talk, but to blurt, and sometimes quite rudely, his profanity acute as a sailor's, though he lives so far from the sea, and from the crude ilk of seamen.

I neared a bluff above the river and found him digging. With the same stick, he poked at a box turtle, hoping, I suppose, to make it move. When he saw me, he shrunk down as much as the turtle was shrunken into itself just below him.

"I will not harm you, Caleb," I said to his arched back. "I am Nell Doerr. Out hunting fossils just as you are hunting turtles."

He rose up then from all fours, his head jerking from side to side. He dropped the stick he had used to torment the turtle.

"Come here," I said. "Come look." I opened my rucksack and held out a piece of Pennsylvanian rock with a small, lacy fossil bryozoan spread across the top. He approached, hesitant, as though I might hurt him, his arm outstretched. I let him take the fossil. Behind him, the relieved turtle scurried into the grass.

"Fossil," Caleb said. He touched the white lace. "Fossil," he said again. He was filthy, from matted hair, to torn shirt, to tattered trousers. His feet were bare.

"Bryozoan," I said slowly.

He looked at me then, his large mouth widening into a grin. He peered into my eyes and I could see a human soul. A spark. Then he dropped the rock and ran.

This evening, as I went to shut and bar the door, I found two stones in my doorway. I knew them immediately to be Caleb's offerings. Two Pennsylvanian rocks, each containing a lacy fan of bryozoan fossil. Before I shut my door, before I barred myself into my house for the night, I stood on my porch. "Thank you!" I shouted, my voice lifting. "Thank you!"

Diary Entry

Caleb has taken an old flannel shirt and sewn the sleeve cuffs together to make a strap to hang over his shoulder. Sewn into a rough bag, this makeshift tote holds the many rocks he finds. It holds my discoveries, as well, for he willingly carries them to spare me the labor.

How quickly he has learned the color palette of Pennsylvanian rock. How quickly he has learned in what layers to concentrate his searches. How quickly he has divided the various shapes that make up bryozoan fossils. Filthy, stooped, jerking, shy, unwilling to be touched. He is all these, yes. But he seems to have a genius for color, shape, and the wonderful naming we do together.

"Fenestrellina," we say as we walk.

"Fenestella," I say, and he repeats. Sometimes he marches, like a little soldier, and we take turns: "Fistulipora, three, four. Prismopora, three, four. Streblotrypa, three, four. Stenopora, three, four. Rhombopora, three, four. Stomatopora, three, four. Diploporaria." His arms lose their jerkiness, and he swings them rhythmically as he walks. "Penniretepara. Archimedes, three, four. Constellaria, three, four. Leioclema, three, four. Thamniscus, three, four." And then we start all over again. Already, in a month, he has found each of these bryozoans. He has never allowed me to pat him, but he smiles shyly when I hold his offerings, and he accepts my congratulations and my genuine praise for his ability to discover. Of course he comes and goes as he pleases, perhaps still spending much of his time tormenting turtles. Or catching squirrels—he attached a bushy tail, rather odiferous, to his hat last week. Or perhaps his mother can settle him to some household tasks occasionally. When he arrives—never at my home when I am setting out or returning, but rather always when I am mid-journey—I welcome him. "Caleb," I call out to him. "My most brilliant boy."

On this day I happened upon him, rather than him upon me, at a bluff that has yielded bryozoan fossils to us. I walked up behind him, where he seemed to be studying something in his hand. On hearing me he quickly shoved the something in his pocket. A glimmer of sunshine caught it before he could secret it away. Solomon's watch, found, of course, by one who is so adept at finding. I tamped my impulse to question him, for he would feel my intensity as anger rather than relief. He had found the watch, after all, just as he found turtles and fossils, trinkets and coins, medicine bottles and handkerchiefs. Was it mine to claim, or his to have? I wasn't certain. I remained silent, though I longed to touch the watch, to take it again into my possession, to have that keepsake.

I cared for Caleb more.

Diary Entry

Today I have had a visit from Caleb's mother, Sarah Cunningham. She stood in my doorway holding two of Caleb's finds, rocks embedded with archimedes. "He carries stones with him. He blurts nonsense. He says your name, 'Doerr, Doerr, Doerr,' over and over again. What have you done to him?"

I invited her in. She hesitated. Am I so frightening? But she followed me inside, where I bid her sit in my one comfortable chair. Her eyes lingered on the table, covered with the fossils I was preparing to ship to Smith. "These will be studied in our Nation's capital," I said to Mrs. Cunningham. "Caleb's fossils among them."

She asked me to explain myself, and I did, a patient teacher, more patient than I had to be with Caleb, even, for Caleb never questioned what he found. He needed no explanation of what process formed a fossil, what a fossil might tell us about the age of the earth, about our earth then as compared to now, about how science and study might illuminate the process of how we ourselves might have come into being, about the process of finding, naming, piecing together. I showed the indelible patterns and pieces that represented what she had called the blurting of nonsense. Unlike Caleb, she refused to attempt the words. She refused to touch the rocks I held out to her.

When I finished, she said, simply, "You have bewitched my son."

"I have given his wanderings a purpose, Sarah Cunningham," I said. "He has a genius. Some of his discoveries have matched my own."

"He is my son," said Sarah. She stood. "I do not want him to participate in your science. Your study. It goes against the Bible. Against God."

"I assure you I have said nothing that might undermine Caleb's faith." I did not wish to discuss her son's obvious incomprehension, his inability to grasp the

most basic tenets of either religion or science. The boy is completely unschooled, unfettered, and treated by most as closer to savage than human. I had at least found a glimmer of comprehension, a spark that connected him to mission. "I will pay him. No, I will pay you, for each of his discoveries that I deem worthy enough to study or ship to the National Museum."

She nodded her head. Smiled briefly in spite of herself. "I will credit his finds," I said.

Her eyes widened, then narrowed. "You will not. Do not use his name." She placed the rocks she had brought, Caleb's discoveries, on the table. "Are these worthy of study?" she asked.

I did not examine them. I went to my room, to my drawer, and found a gold piece. Sarah Cunningham left with what she had likely come for in the first place.

Diary Entry

I leave tomorrow for the return to Kansas, and already I miss my Arkansas home, where everything is so green, and light dapples the roadways through the leaves of trees. The scent of pine, the clear water, the trickling sounds of springs, the soft needles and spongy ground of the lowlands, all of these are the setting of my growing up. I will even miss the grunting of Father Robert's hogs, but especially the neighing of his horses, the soft thudding of their hooves as they frisk in the corral, jostle each other for hay. Something about a place must always be part of our minds and hearts, to create such yearning.

Oh, Solomon, I yearn for you as well. Your laughter was like no other's, deep and grumbling, twice the laugh because so suppressed, so forced to bubble up your throat and geyser forth like an Arkansas spring. And nobody could lift such an eyebrow when asking a question, or expressing skepticism. Nobody cracked knuckles with a greater snap, nor groaned so when putting on boots. I still hear your voice, and especially when I return to Arkansas, where we courted, so shy at first, then with bold expression of honest feelings. People die; feelings do not. We move to another landscape, yet the familiar is ever lodged in our hearts.

Kansas, with its sky and miles and miles of prairie, also has a place in my heart. Sunshine, wind, violent weather, all opening to vista, to distance. I see the miles ahead I have yet to travel in Kansas, and that speeds my journey, grounds me in time. The oases of tree-lined creeks, the wide and muddy Wakarusa, Kansas, and Missouri rivers that ooze rather than run, the red-winged blackbirds and finches and meadowlarks always scattering skyward, and the flaky outcroppings of rock that yield so much of the life of the past—all these things live in me, and call to me, when I am in Arkansas, and I miss them. My two places, both with a Kansas in them. I belong in each place. I live in each place, am alive in each place.

Here, I am with my Solomon. And Benjamin and Lawrence, our two lost boys. Our hearts fill as we grow older. Sometimes I feel full to bursting. I am sentimental tonight, perhaps because I return to Kansas tomorrow.

Letter from Sally Miller

Tuesday, August 4, 1874
Waverly, MO

Dearest Nell—

I write to you in haste, for I am closely watched. I found, yesterday, the cache of your letters, sent to me over the past four years and secreted from me by Horace. Though my eyes well with tears as I write to you, I dare not cry—he listens as closely as he watches. Nell, he has taken hard to drink, and has become hard because of it. I am forbidden to leave the house, where he has made me prisoner. I am not even allowed church anymore, for some of my friends have taken up temperance, working toward the prohibition of alcohol. The only prohibitions I know now are the ones that Horace imposes on me.

Would that we could correspond, but he will hide your letters from me. Would that you could visit me, but few come and go from this house. Would that I could flee to you, but he would know, and find me. I will give this letter to the boy, now man, who once accompanied me on my lepidoptera expeditions—he now works occasionally for us. The other day, as he carried stove wood into the house, he said to me softly, "Smoke finds its way out, to mix with air." He knows how much my freedom to collect butterflies has meant to me. Horace has, of course, read the letters you sent, and though he has not spoken of them, I am certain that he thinks ill of the consolation and fine advice you offered. He is jealous of all friendship, now that he has lost all his friends.

Please remember just this one thing before I close—you are near to my heart. Not a day goes by that I don't remember our friendship and the few blessed times we have shared company. I try for patience. One of my late mother's oft-spoken pieces of advice was, "This too shall pass." Unfortunately, I believe she was forced to say it much too often in her life. Pray for me, Nell. Pray for Horace, as I certainly do, for I will not allow his flinty heart to spark anger or hatred in mine. Do not try to write until I next write you—another letter will only upset what peace I can often manage.

I hear Horace pacing below, and must close.

Fondly,
Sally Miller

Sunday Lesson, Prepared for
the Ladies of the Unitarian Church

August 1875

My dear friends, I thank you for the invitation to speak to you today. I take as my topic creatures that most likely none of us has seen. Byrozoans, and in particular moss bryozoans. I have seen them as fossils, and I bring with me this evening a variety of the discoveries I've made here in Lawrence and in the Eastern Kansas region.

(Show no more than eight specimens—do not get carried away with details and science.)

Besides noting the structure of bryozoans, their varieties and their parts, my true mission tonight is to share my thoughts about these creatures and what they might tell us about ourselves. The organism we call moss bryozoan is created of one-celled creatures that gather together. They congregate, they build together, and they begin to differentiate from each other, each one taking on—with the help of thousands, no millions, of others—the important functions of a living creature. Some act as fanlike tentacles that are able to stir the water around them, while others act as filters so that they might find the food particles in a warm ocean. Still others act as mouth, as digestive tract, as organs of reproduction, and so forth. Each of these parts serves the whole. Just as these cells congregate for their mutual advantage, each finding its own role in creation, so, too, do bryozoans colonize, that a vast stretch of shallow ocean floor might be carpeted with these creatures.

What does this tell us about ourselves? How much like women are these creatures. We are individuals, but each of us understands the strength that comes when we congregate, when each individual talent thrives in a group in a way that makes all of us thrive. Those among us who study go forth to teach. Those with a talent for organization make certain of the wheres, whys, and whens so that we might gather. Those who nurture in difficult circumstances sit with the sick and aged, and in death sit in solemn black, strengthening each other in our losses. Those of us who do not cook well fashion cloth into magnificent garments. Those of us who are awkward with a needle find a talent in our gardens and with our chickens.

Collectively, and only collectively, do we remember the details of our lives—the extended families, the birthdays and anniversaries, the struggles and triumphs, the courtships and further studies of far-flung children, the travels, the habits, the preferences, and the needs of all of us. What would we be without each other? And what are we together: a whole creature, this assemblage tonight, feeding and fending for each other.

Bryozoans are said to be delicate creatures. As resourceful as they are, if the conditions around them change, they can find themselves unable to function. They might suffer a change in temperature—too warm or too frigid—or a receding water level that strands them in drought. Any number of causes might kill an entire colony of bryozoans. Then, if conditions favor it, they might be eventually discovered one day as their fossilized selves.

Being simple, however, being made up of one-celled organisms, bryozoans are adaptable. In newly favorable climates and conditions, those cells begin to gather, multiply, differentiate, compound themselves, and colonize. Hence bryozoans, though found only in fossil forms here in Kansas, are still found in warm, shallow shorelines all over the globe along with their cousins, the corals.

This adaptability, this resilience, also reminds me of women. How often we have suffered loss, through disease and war and drought. How often we have had to begin again in a new environment. How often we have been torn apart and then come together to rebuild our community. Many of you in this room will remember the sacking of Lawrence by Sheriff Samuel Jones, will remember the devastating raid of William C. Quantrill, will remember the difficulties our men suffered because of the Civil War, and more recently because of the failures in our national economy. We may be delicate creatures, but together we have withstood much, and we have come to thrive. Out of near extinction we have persisted. Lawrence women, we are bryozoan—we have those same powers of survival, of renewal. That, my dear friends, is why I celebrate bryozoans and plan to continue to discover them in all their numbers. Thank you for the opportunity to talk with you tonight.

Letter from Sally Miller

Tuesday, March 14, 1876
Waverly, MO

Dear Nell—

I have done it. Finally. The thumb has been lifted. Or, should I say, I have lifted the thumb.

Perhaps you have been a part of this liberation, as well, if it was you who made sure that Hugh Cameron stopped on his inaugural march to Washington and stayed, sitting with Horace night after night, coaxing him through a tremens delirious enough to nearly shatter him. And yet he remains whole.

Or was it you who suggested that Smith write to him imploring some specimens from my collection for the Philadelphia Exposition? Oh, Nell, I am prisoner no longer, because Horace is no longer prisoner of his demon—the drink that would surely have killed him. The world can be a changing and changed place. Even today I am readying work—sketches and butterflies—for display beginning May 10. I unpin my specimens, as I have been unpinned, to ship, each in a tiny box, stacked together in a large crate, safely making their way to what will surely be an exhibition to outdo all exhibitions. And in my own small way, I will be there, too.

Nell, I cannot believe my good fortune. I hear the Fairmount Park displays will include a new device of communication by a Mr. Bell, and some of the inventions of Mr. Edison that the newspaper reports. The gift of Liberty, as well, a torch-bearing arm sent from France. Such tribute lights my own sense of freedom, though I am certain I will never see the great arm beyond the sketches already published in *Leslie's Weekly*. Yes, I read newspapers and magazines again. I attend church. I have returned to the fold of the WCTU, unafraid to recount my own horrible experiences, my own story of Horace and his changings. You may write me with the knowledge that I will receive your words, unread by my husband. You may at some time even be allowed a visit, or I a visit to you, though, just as the chrysalis is vulnerable when first emerging from the cocoon as butterfly, I must beware of thinking that all will be a steady course toward light out of the darkness that has submerged me these several years.

Tentatively, then, I move into air, take such deep breaths, and begin to look forward to life anew.

Your friend—
Sally

Letter to Sister Mary

Friday, April 21, 1876
Lawrence, KS

Dearest Mary—

You will remember how many slaves, ill-clothed, unbathed, down in spirit, we secreted beneath the barn. If we hadn't divined the spirit that lurked in them, that pushed them to run from their masters and the abominations of slavery, we would have thought them little above the cattle in our field, the hogs in our pen. They were seen as such by their masters, who used every power over them—whip and lash and chains—except for the power of love that might recognize their humanity. Mary, to be reduced to but one thing—"slave," "woman," "idiot"—and to be judged by that one thing alone.

To my point. Today I testified in court for the humanity of a thirteen-year-old boy, Caleb Cunningham. I have mentioned him in my letters as my companion in the finding of bryozoan fossils. He is mentally challenged, of course—as are his poor mother and his two brothers and three sisters. But he the most severely. His physical maturity has beset him, and he, like many other boys and men, has difficulty in controlling his impulses. He has been seen in public with a swollen manhood. He has followed young women home, "leering." He "attacked" Rebecca Stoller and Ramonia Withers on a picnic outing, though they withstood no physical harm.

His own mother had him brought before the court to be declared insane, an idiot, and, as such, she petitioned his commitment to the Kansas State Insane Asylum in Osawatomie, the town made famous by Captain John Brown when he lived in Kansas.

Mary, what could I say? I did not say the worst, that one day I happened upon him at one of our bluffs, a favorite for revealing fossils, and saw him in onanistic pleasure. He did not see me. I did not say that, as he has matured, his body thickening, his voice deepening, I have felt at times unsettled. I did not say that his mother and siblings have taken no responsibility for him or any of his actions for the three years I have known him. I did not say that such a trial, in which a thirteen-year-old boy is made criminal for having a feeble brain, is itself an altogether unjust, humiliating, and feebleminded business.

I did say that Caleb displays an intelligence, an acumen, an ability for hunting and finding fossils that is almost inexplicable given his upbringing, circumstances, and education, that he needs supervision, and forces of control, and stability, but that a trial, a judgement, a sentencing all reduce him to but one thing—"idiot"—for the rest of his life. Who would want to be but one thing? "Judge Parker," I asked, "are you not father, husband, business owner, deacon, Republican, former Mayor, and sinner all at once?"

He accused me of impertinence. I pleaded guilty. "But," I retorted, "only because of the injustice about to be levied upon a young man still a child. None of us should be labeled but one thing for an entire life. It is a blessing in life when we outlive that one thing we might have been known for, especially when unsavory."

Mary, Caleb is but a fatherless boy caught between two worlds—youth and adulthood—who has had no guidance toward self-control and self-regulation. His mother admitted that she has not brought him to church service since he was seven years old, as he was so often deemed disruptive. And so I was disruptive today.

I am sorry to harangue. You know my passions. I hope that you still share them, though all of the circumstances of your life temper them. Sometimes I envy you. Michael must be such a comfort, and you have Sara and John and all the joys and complications of their lives. I have no one to nurture. My work yet sustains me. I am with the stones, but my heart is not stone.

I splotch this letter with inexplicable tears. Forgive me.

Your loving sister,
Nell

Letter from Hugh Cameron

Dear Nell Johnson Doerr—

As ever, I am your comrade in pursuits others might find beyond the realm of their understanding. No matter that I am reviled, I persist in my crusade for Temperance. Our Nation's Capital, I swear, will never be temperate, if the recent inaugural is any indication. Such public drunkenness! and Rutherford B. Hayes is not one to make laws to curtail anyone's behavior. I spoke out for the working man, and for the inclusion of God in the lives of men, all to no avail.

Although you and I do not agree on all matters of politics and religion, we are equals, perhaps, in being suspect—according to others—and because we follow our own directions, wherever we might be led. My inaugural trek did indeed, as you requested, lead me to Horace Miller, poor man, though I had not known, before I saw him, the terrible grip alcohol had on his heart and mind and soul. Such a vise is not easily loosened, but being complete in his misery, he allowed me to help. I simply sat beside him, as one might sit next to a child awakening from a frightful dream. We drank buckets of coffee and tea and water, we sang "The Battle Hymn of the Republic" over and over. We gave sermons, ranting as we are wont to do, on the evils perpetrated by small minds everywhere. Yes, we also prayed.

Finally, his mind enlarged enough to push away his terrible desire—even need—for the bottle. I continued my journey, with a short detour to the Missouri Statehouse in Jefferson City, where I delivered a letter from our great Kansas prohibition crusader John St. John to the Missouri Governor and Legislative bodies. Of course I had copies of the same letter for Hayes and for the Senate and House—a nest of drunkards both.

On my return trip I found Horace and Sally Miller to be faring well. I take no real credit for the man's revival, for such conversion comes from within or not at all. If I was an instrument, as you imply in your note to me, I am happy to be considered so.

I continue to find fossils of the kind you collect, or should I venture that they find me, for I do not actively pursue them. Should you happen upon a box of rocks on your porch someday, consider the contents as my gift to you. Do not worry, they will be properly labeled and logged as much as I am able. I am off on another trek soon, this time to New Mexico with former Senator Ross, with whom I have not always been on good terms, though I regret my part in the public excoriation of him for his vote against the impeachment of Johnson. Ross is interested in the Southwestern territories. Unfortunately, we will go by carriage.

Your faithful servant,
General Hugh Cameron, Kansas Hermit

Letter to Stepfather Robert Johnson

Monday, June 26, 1876
Lawrence, KS

Dear Father Robert:

The first time you hoisted me onto Molly's back, and instructed me to clutch her mane, and stepped away, and clicked your tongue—was I three years old? two?—and she paced the corral, two circles before you stopped her, you said to me, "Nell, my girl, you were born to ride."

So determined you were that I would be comfortable on horseback. I remember your pride, telling Mother Jo, "She has the instinct." I did not know what instinct was, but I knew it was important to you, and to horses, and it brought me to share your admiration for good stock and for being good with the stock.

How many days did I spend alone with the horses, and then with Mary and the horses? When you lifted Mary onto Molly I remembered so clearly my very first ride, what it felt like to be on top of, but also almost part of, a huge creature. I lifted Hiram onto Molly, and I thank you for letting me. As we grew, how we three rode. Days on horseback, with errands into town, or with nothing but time and distance to pass through.

Mother Jo wrote to me of the death of Molly's line. I remember that none of her fillies—Betsy, Smoke, and Mist (how I loved each of them)—ever had more than one of her own that you could deem fit to become a breeding mare. I know you had hopes for Mist, but she only gave you one foal, and now that one—Mother Jo said you named her Molly, too, with hopes that she could fulfill that name—has died trying to give birth, the colt stillborn. I am sorry for the news.

I have not produced grandchildren for you either, though Hiram and Mary keep your line intact. I never knew if my first mother and father had brothers and sisters, so I suppose that line may be at its end as well. Or perhaps not. Bloodlines have less importance to me every day, perhaps because I have no children, or perhaps because you and Mother Jo taught me that nurturing and love, sustenance and growth, do not depend on blood alone.

You will remember that I nurtured Caleb, the mentally deficient boy who wandered nearly feral through the countryside. He had a knack for fossil finding, and for three years I believed I was helping to give his meanderings, given the neglect of others, a purpose. I paid his mother when he made significant finds, and she became used to knocking on my door.

When the boy was judged mentally incompetent and sent to the Kansas State Insane Asylum, I thought Mrs. Cunningham's visits would stop, but she came with the hope I might train one of her girls, as I had Caleb. I did not train Caleb—he came to his skill through instinct—but the daughter, Catherine, had no eye, no sense of what she was looking for or where she might find the bryozoan fossils that Caleb had recognized as though they were treasured friends. I sent her home within hours, and Sarah Cunningham knocked, wishing Catherine to be paid for the trouble of spending a morning with me.

Within a fortnight four gold pieces went missing from the drawer in my desk. Father Robert, I mounted the finest, fastest horse at Fry & Russell's Livery, and I was told which wagon Sarah had taken, and in what direction, and that she had been gone half the morning. Less than an hour revealed Mrs. Cunningham and her daughter on the Baldwin Road. She reined in her horse upon hearing my galloping hooves approach from behind.

"My gold," I said simply.

She flushed, red-faced with what I hoped was shame.

"I deserve to go see him," she said. "It was you put him there."

Father Robert, a greater untruth has rarely been told me. She had nobody else to blame, I suppose. I told her the truth. My truth, at least, as I've written you and Mary before. I held out my hand. "My gold," I repeated.

"Spent on supplies," said Sarah, motioning to the provisions in the back of the wagon. I kicked my horse and surged ahead of her. The power of the horse, I thought, might convince her of my resolve, and when I rode back at her, the livery nag shied, nearly upsetting the wagon. Mrs. Cunningham shied, too. She took a small bag from under the wagon seat, placed it on her lap, and opened it.

"Give it to me," I said. When she refused, I moved the horse closer and snatched the bag from her. I reached inside. Gold pieces, yes. Two of them. And a silver watch, on a silver chain, with the initials *SD* etched on the casing. "I suspected that Caleb had found my watch," I said. I held it to my cheek.

"But that is my watch. From my father, Simon Dooley. The only thing of his I have."

Though her voice was plaintive, I knew her to be a liar. I put the gold pieces and the watch in my saddlebag then threw her empty purse at her. I would have helped her, Father Robert, had she asked me. "I send Caleb my very best regards," I said. I asked her never to darken my doorway again unless she expected great consequences.

In my frustration I galloped back to the livery, that fine horse under me, lifting me, and lifting my spirits. You know how a fast ride on a good horse can bring you back to life, and bring you close to memory—of all the fine horses and the spirited moments shared. You taught me that. In but forty-two minutes, according to Solomon's watch, I returned the fine horse to Fry & Russell's.

I hope you thrive in spite of your loss. With hope, you will, as you always have, find another mare worthy of your time and efforts with her. I send my love to you, to Mother Jo, to Hiram and Mary, and to all of theirs as well.

Your daughter,
Nell

Diary Entry

I am far from Philadelphia, yet I feel that I am there, for Smith has written that three of my bryozoan specimens are on display as examples of fossil finds in the West. He writes, "They will not arrest the attention of our Western Kansas mosasaur, shipped here by Sternberg, but they are all part of the record we are accumulating that will someday help us understand the great Inland Sea of which Kansas was once a part." That is reassurance enough for me, for sometimes the meek do inherit the earth. Mosasaurs are now extinct. Bryozoans still live in oceans everywhere, and thus more intimately link us to evolution. And where my fossils are displayed, so are Sally Miller's butterflies. In some small way, we are together as well.

Letter from Mother Jo

Thursday, September 7, 1876
Pine Bluff, AR

My Dear Nell—

Brace yourself for hard news. Your dear Father Robert has passed from this world. I cannot piece together exact circumstances. He was horseback when he left home for town—this was Monday of the past week. He crawled home, badly bruised, bleeding from his head, from his mouth, from a crushed shoulder. He could not speak. His horse has not yet returned, and I do not expect he will. Your Father Robert was brave in his passing. Oh, Nell, he held my hand so tight I still feel the squeezing of his fingers, as though he was trying to pour himself and all the strength of his body into mine. How can a man so crushed and bruised smile through the end?

We assume he was thrown from his horse. John Rudd, he called him— that stud was one of his wildest, yet he insisted John Rudd would be another of his fine animals. Now we have neither him nor the animal. I digress in delivering terrible news and then speaking only my thoughts, for you have lost someone dear to you as well.

Please return to Pine Bluff as soon as possible. We will bury him tomorrow—his coffin was in the house this last night. His dear face, which never fails to bring me to tears, is at rest. We will wait for you before we memorialize him. Mary and Hiram send you their love, as do their families. We huddle together in our grief, and need only you to complete our circle. Nell, I never thought to see this day so soon. To see the burial plot growing, with the loss of such a fine man as your Father Robert. I am bewildered by his death. So are his grandchildren—Sara's Charles is but five, and Henry just three. Neither understands what is happening, and baby Francis is happily oblivious, though occasionally he lets forth a torrent of wailing, as though shrieking for us all. Hiram, as you know, is stoical, yet the set look on his face gives way to spasms of trembling. I tell him, "Even grown men are allowed to be babies." Penelope and the girls sit close at his side, and I know their presence is a comfort. Little Jacob—he will ever be called that for being born so late—is trying to be a little man like his father. You never saw such a grimace on the face of one so young.

Nell, I need you. Do let us know you will be coming to us right away. I know it is hard to journey the miles, but once here you will be welcomed with a joy as deep as our sorrow at Father Robert's death. He was the love of my life, as Solomon was yours. I know you were severed from that great abiding much sooner than I. Because of that, you have more experience in widowhood than I. We can be of comfort to each other, we who have lost what we have loved most.

Your loving Mother Jo

Diary Entry

I leave Pine Bluff with more regret than usual, for one more loved one is buried in Arkansas. I can never return to quite the same family. Father Robert is properly memorialized, and well-remembered. Born as he was in 1803, he lived a long life, though the circumstances of his death are uncharacteristic. A better horseman cannot be found in Arkansas or Tennessee. He once rode from Pleasant View, Tennessee, the place of his birth—and Mother Jo's—into what is now Texas, and across the Rio Grande, and then back again, nearly nine months horseback, with adventures he told again and again, though not to boast. He was always wanting to teach—independence, courage, hope, persistence, and love. What great tales he wove.

Woven into that story is my own, though now I hear it accurately, from Mother Jo, for the first time. Father Robert always said, and I can hear his voice, "That leads me to you, my little skedaddle. Jo and I riding like the wind, loping toward our freedom from her outlaw brothers and father, ready to cross the Hatchie by ferry, run by your father Charles Onnen, but that wasn't to be. Someone had burned the cabin. Jo heard your cries. A miracle you were still alive. She found you in the ashes, took you to her breast. What could we do but rescue you, your parents gone? So we hurried you to Memphis where we had friends. Wrote letters back but never heard of living relatives. You were meant to start again, just as we were, in this good country." And so it stood.

Mother Jo, perhaps in facing the death of her husband and knowing of the damnable death of my Solomon, was more forthcoming. They were indeed riding from Pleasant View, wondering if they were followed. Mother Jo had indeed lost a child to miscarriage. They rode up to my family cabin to find it smoldering to

146

ash. My father had been hung with the ferry rope from a tree a small distance into the woods. Mother Jo heard a sound like a lost fledgling. She searched in the blackened rubble. More sound, and Father Robert jumped into a room more intact and found my mother, dead, hair singed, clothing steaming, and yet they saw me moving underneath, protected rather than smothered. My mother did that for me. Saved my life. Mother Jo did indeed take me to her breast, though Father Robert thought her touched in her belief that she might produce milk for me. Yet she did. And they rode away with me quickly, for my father obviously had made enemies—Charles Onnen took advantage of those needing to cross the river, Father Robert told her—and, of course, Mother Jo's family was likely at the chase. They did write letters, but never heard another thing. "Oh, Nell," said Mother Jo, "you were the best thing that could have happened to us. Saved by your mother as though she knew we would be there soon. I hope she knew that."

Such grief we carry. We hope, we discover, we love. We also despair, and destroy, and burn to the ground. Such was Quantrill and his raiders. I have lost much. So, now, has Mother Jo. I leave with the touch of tombstone, to seek the touch of fossil rock. Each contains the story of something once living, now dead.

I return, having lost two fathers, to a place where I lost my husband. Yet I will take solace from the warm embraces of those still living, those so dear to me, those who would shelter me as my own mother did, and nurture me as Mother Jo did, with hope, discovery, and love.

Diary Entry

Sally Miller climbed into the railcar and waved from the window until the train pulled away. I have returned to what feels like an empty house. Perhaps that feeling is mutual, for though she returns to a husband seemingly reformed, she still feels isolated and alone, empty in all but her collecting, drawing, and studying. These things fill my life, as well, for we are companions in those pursuits. Her wariness worries me. Horace has been good to her, but in the way of courtship rather than marriage. "When will the marriage begin again?" she asked.

During the worst he was physically violent. Her left arm, twisted to permanent damage, hangs straight, and she has trouble lifting her hand high enough to button the top of her dress. I did that for her, though she confessed that at home she executes the task painfully, rather than asking Horace, who might be either angered or shamed by the memory of his abuse of her. She is giddy with his change, but that alternates with a darkness that comes from the memory of all she's experienced. She is, in some ways, diminished, as are so many women in her position. "When happiness comes simply from not being afraid, is it truly happiness?" she asked. Her expectations are indeed lowered. Having a husband whose virtue is displayed in his not mistreating himself or you, well, that is not the same as having a companion to comfort you on the journey. Would that she weren't childless. Though I have no living children, and have come to accept that, Sally Miller, had she a daughter, might have the kind of soothing companion she misses in a husband. "We expect so little," she said just last night. "Does that mean we become so little?"

I assured her that I expected much of her, and expected her to be much, in spite of all circumstances. Women's lives might someday expand. Hadn't we both had pieces of our collection displayed at the Exposition? Hadn't we both had correspondence with respected scientific minds? Weren't we both learning beyond the expectations required of Woman? Weren't we finding some sense of independence for ourselves, whether husbandless, like me, or working in spite of husband? Didn't we aspire to more—to more study, more discovery, perhaps even presenting our findings somewhere?

In reassuring Sally Miller, I was perhaps instead making her feel what her limitations might be upon returning home, for she seemed glum this morning, and tears welled in her good-bye to me from the platform. I am saddened that though we laughed, walked about, took our meals together, attended the Unitarian fellowship, and met so many fine people, Sally proving herself a kind soul among kind souls, our time together might have sharpened the pain of her return to a wary life. I mean to help. Sometimes I cannot.

Diary Entry

Home again after a week of travel by train, buggy, horse, and foot. A pleasant ride on the Leavenworth, Lawrence & Fort Gibson railway to Baldwin City, where I was met by my sometimes correspondent Anthony Hale, who has made fossil discoveries in the Adams Quarry in Douglas County, and near his residence in that comely town. He showed me the display case dedicated to local fossils at Baker [University].* We rode by horseback to those places that have yielded him fossils, and I found a fistolipora worth packing into my bag. Hale's wife Eleanor was a most cordial hostess, who served a sumptuous dinner and an equally fine supper.

The Baldwin City extension took me through a rain-drenched landscape to Ottawa. Eleanor and Mr. Hale rode along to introduce me to their colleague, Dr. Archibald Purcell, a professor in the sciences at the Baptist university there. The main building is nearly as impressive as Parmenter Hall in Baldwin City. Wherever I travel, Kansas shows its desire for education. A Kansas city, it seems, is not fully a city without its university, its opera house, and its dozens of churches. Spires everywhere, and alongside them the stout, square university halls. Purcell is an energetic man who fairly spiders his way along bluffs and stream beds. His finds did not surprise me, though they are rare; a Septopora, for example, that rivals any of my discoveries. With his lively eye and almost frantic pace, he seems to want everything at once. After a morning of labor, we ate well at a dining establishment near the university, and Hale and Purcell saw me to the depot, where Anthony met Eleanor for their return to Baldwin City, and Archibald Purcell secured for me a coach to Osawatomie.

A detour of twenty-five miles, with rough travel, to be sure, with an arrival

---

* The oldest in Kansas, founded in 1858 by the Methodist Church.

well past supper. On the way I reached my hand into my satchel for reassurance more than once. The rock I had brought for Caleb, one of his most important finds, lay waiting, as did I, to see him. When I marched up to the main building of the insane asylum the next day, I shivered with the atmosphere of the place. It was not the bars on the windows, nor the few employees on the grounds who stared at me; it was not the imposing structure, nor the anticipation of witnessing the lives of so many lost souls; it was not the prospect of visiting Caleb. No, it was the knowledge of restraint, the lack of freedom, the solid insularity and boundaries of the place that closed over my heart and shivered it with grief.

I set aside all trepidation and inquired at the office after Caleb Cunningham. Had they received my letter? Yes, and they'd written that I might not be welcome, that I might interrupt their efforts in working with Caleb, to keep him stable. "But I am here," I insisted. "At some effort and expense."

I asked if he had been visited in the months since his arrival and was told he had not. He was working in the fields, I was told, some distance away.

"I am used to walking," I declared.

With a sigh, the administrator called for a young attendant and directed the man to take me to the potato field. We walked but half a mile when I saw the contingent of "wards of the state," as they called them, digging in the ground. Harvesting potatoes in moist soil, so that each potato looked like a clod of earth, piled in heaps at the end of each row. At one of the rows, Caleb's row, I planted myself and waited. He saw me. I believe he recognized me, as his body twitched, his head bent in concentration over the potato fork. He continued to dig, but when he had amassed a number more potatoes, he had to carry them toward me. He approached, his face as muddy and expressionless as the potatoes he carried.

I met him with an offering in my fist. "I am Nell Doerr," I said, my hand outstretched. He knew who I was, of course, but I met him as I'd first met him. "I will not harm you, Caleb Cunningham. I have been digging fossils, just as you are digging potatoes." I opened my fist. "Fenestella," I said. I reached toward him. "One of your very best finds. Perhaps you'd like it to remember our time together."

He dropped the potatoes onto the heap. He looked at me without expression. He reached for the rock, but he did not examine it. Instead, he turned and flung it into the air, past the dug furrows of potatoes and into the brown grasses that skirted the field. I stopped the cry in my throat. He marched back to his potato fork, and I recalled the times we'd marched, "blurting nonsense," as his mother said, laughing together. Oh, Caleb.

"Don't think on it, ma'am," said the young attendant. "He's a moody fellow. He don't talk much."

I marched away, leaving the fossil behind, for who knows, he might search for it so that he might please himself, if not me, in finding it once more.

Carriage and train again, and the whole time my thoughts on a boy who once smiled, bending to rock and really seeing, and knowing the names of what he saw, and knowing his own name, and worth. How tenderly he might pluck the rock from the grass, and carry it to his room, and find a place for it next to his bed, near his miserable heart.

Home again.

Diary Entry

This town, this Lawrence, is ever about Progress. Railroads, bridges, banks, windmills, opera houses. I sometimes wonder if people remember how, at the end of the war, we celebrated modestly, even chastely, our victory over the South, satisfied with our role as abolitionist K. T., as Free State Kansas. We sacrificed the lives of our soldiers in the Union cause, we made martyrs of men in Quantrill's Raid, we gave our new towns and counties the names of the great men of the struggle.

Now we name everything for merchants, for our new god is Progress. Some progress has made my work easier. The railroad blasts anything in its path, exposing fossils in newly created bluffs. Everywhere, quarries are being dug for stone for new buildings, and new fossils are discovered. Just last year Mudge noticed a fossilized amphibian footprint exposed in a curbing stone on Kansas Avenue in Topeka, and he traced it to the quarry of Crane & Dodd in Osage.

On the other hand, this new dam has ruined my fossil hunting along the river. The floods of last year churned up mud and sand and would have made new to human eyes the world of eons ago, rediscovered. This damming of the Kansas River, for power, has rendered me powerless. The river widens, backs up. Where there were sandbars, there is shallow water, stretching bank to bank upstream for perhaps a mile or more, the river waiting patiently to pass over the dam, the water checked in order that we might mill flour.

I must walk upstream, inconvenienced to be sure, but also frustrated at treasures lost, a past flooded and thus buried, scientific progress checked that a merchant might have a better chance for profit. What good to spread from sea to shining sea, as have the railroads, dictating a pathway to commerce, if we do not understand the past, the natural world that preceded ours? We fly across the earth on iron wheels, we gouge the earth with iron plows, we flood the rivers with our barriers of iron pylons, all in the name of profit. We do not profit. We build iron bars wherein we are prisoners of ambition rather than people of understanding. We desire money rather than richness.

I am tired from my long walk of the day, an unprofitable day, cold and windy. I had no good finds on the lonely sandbar. My feet, still wet, are but chilled bone.

Letter from Sally Miller

Sunday, October 13, 1878
Waverly, MO

Dear Nell—

I have arrived home safely, and found it safe. I thank you for your generous hospitality. Your lovely home, with your wide porch, is made lovelier by your activity in it. Yes, you confess to lack of prowess in domestic matters, but I was well fed, well taken care of, well pleased with the entirety of my journey to you, and with you. I have often told you of the salvation your friendship has been, a beacon of light during that darkest of periods, and now a kind of firelight glow of companionship. Such peace I find in your routines, such beauty in the walks we take, such erudition in your knowledge of what we found in those places you have learned will yield discoveries. Butterflies, too, have patterns, but my creatures are certainly not stationary—I almost envy your science, for which you can narrow your sense of where to look, and, more importantly, where not to look.

Some news that will help calm any lingering fears you might have for me. Horace has announced a new understanding of the advantages to both of us in my being paid for my collecting. He is now helping me find, mount, and ship specimens. He is competitive, yet knows well enough that mine is the knowledge he needs to rely on, even when he wants to insist that he has captured a species never before observed in Missouri. He wants to travel, "tenting," he calls it, so that we might go farther and stay longer in our excursions, finding those enclaves where particular butterflies have made their homes in particular places. In that sense, butterflies might be like your bryozoans, with adaptations according to small changes in climate—temperature, sunlight, rainfall—the same things that favor certain plants over others, so that willows usually weep into water.

Horace's enthusiasm for my world is winning. His passion for politics—through which he failed to find favor, losing the vote for each office he tried to fill, those failures perhaps contributing to his succumbing, as he so fiercely did, to drink—needed some other, more positive outlet. He is as determined to find a previously unrecorded butterfly so that he can contribute to the field of lepidoptery. I believe nothing will stop him in that pursuit. I have an ally, albeit a competitive one, in my husband again.

How pleasant to return from such a comforting time as I had with you, dear friend, to find a companion in my husband. I will write when I have news.

Yours truly,
Sally

Letter to Sister Mary

Wednesday, September 17, 1879 (After the September 15/16 Twenty-Fifth
Anniversary Celebration of the Founding of Lawrence)
Lawrence, KS

Dear Mary—

The Reunion Band sat at attention, Mr. Turnbull with a thin stick for a
baton, which he raised dramatically, and playfully kept raised, making us
anticipate the crack of that first note, that the beginning of the march might
rush into our ears—drums and coronets—like rifle shots. Mary, the high-
light was Mr. Savage's horn, rescued from Quantrill's Raid, playing brightly
to the large gathering at Bismarck Grove. Joseph Savage finds fossils, as I
do. Another brightness.

Over three thousand people crowded Lawrence. Indiana governor George
Julian was greeted with cannon fire—war and high rhetoric always together—
and spoke of the freedom of the slave leading to the freeing of the American
mind. Ex-governor Charles Robinson spoke, claiming the event to be the
proudest moment of his life. Edward Everett Hale claimed we Kansans were
all joined with and unto Massachusetts, like Siamese twins. Our own Julia
Lovejoy, who sent her dispatches from K.T. to the Eastern papers, congratu-
lated us on our part in changing the course of this nation. Walt Whitman, the
long-bearded poet of the Civil War, stood briefly among us.

From the Territorial days forward we have known our special place in
history. From the beginning we have corrected the deficiencies of place, of
social life, of cultivation and culture, of grace toward a better future. Mary,
we live in one world, and imagine it to be another, better world, and strive
until we succeed in making it so.

Fitting, perhaps, that the band chose Sousa, suddenly popular in American music, and his "Revival March," which you'll recognize from when we as girls sang "In the Sweet Bye and Bye." Perhaps we *have* met the beautiful shore. Patriotism is the worship of the idea of a place, and no place has a loftier imagination about itself than the United States of America, even after the terrible war, which rent us in two, which still rends us in two. The slave has been freed, but I cannot agree with Governor Julian that we have freed our American mind.

We are still at war, Mary, a war between how we live and how we might want to live. No more so than in the territories, which is how I will always think of Kansas. Perhaps all of America is territory still, and we are still trying to civilize ourselves toward the loftiness of our founding, from our Jefferson to our Lincoln. We women have yet to gain the right to vote, though our arguments have been reasonable. We have great political influence, through women's clubs and through our efforts with the Woman's Christian Temperance Union. We will manage Prohibition here in Kansas, I am certain, given the thousands who rallied together at this same Bismarck Grove recently. Then, we were incited to live with the imagination of a better day. We correct ourselves toward our ideals.

I sat, looking, I hope, unperturbed. But I was too unconvinced about the past and present of this Kansas to celebrate gleefully. Our task as women, Mary, is to march toward civilization. Yes, our instruments have survived raids, are battered, even as we are. But we have done our best, and we were together survivors of the past with eyes toward the future, and by the end of the day, even I shed tears. For what, I was not certain, though I suspect for Solomon.

Your loving sister,
Nell

Diary Entry

*I read today of the death of Benjamin Franklin Mudge. Professor Benjamin
Mudge, fossil collector, teacher, first State Geologist of Kansas. Benjamin Mudge,
first president of the Kansas Academy. Benjamin Mudge of the legendary fossil
cabinet, long ago donated to the State Agricultural College. Benjamin Mudge,
whose lectures at the University here I sometimes attended, much to my benefit.
His pallbearers were Snow, Popenoe, Savage, and Parker, all keepers of the same
flame. I wish I could have been in Manhattan to pay my respects, but I did not
learn of his passing in time to travel.*

 *I feel strangely that in one man I've lost two fellow travelers at once. In our
first journey together he was an abolitionist at Quindaro. His home was a fortress
against those who would try to wrest away the slaves he sheltered there. Solomon
and I took from him the slave Maryemma and her three children, hid them in our
wagon, and made the trip to Leavenworth and safety. At that time his profession
was in the law. His passion, though, was in nature, hence his constant study of
geology, his expeditions, his appointment to professor at the State Agricultural
College. He was Samuel's teacher, and hence, in some sense, mine, although he,
like Samuel, was more interested in vertebrates, and made significant discoveries
in Western Kansas, sending them to Marsh at Yale, as does Savage. He was
enthusiastic about any collector, and any collection. I draw out the note Mudge
once wrote, after hearing from Smith of my bryozoan research, congratulating me
on my persistence, my patience, and wishing me well. He hoped we might sometime meet. We had met, but so many years ago that he did not remember our
encounter. Of course, we did not use our actual names, Solomon and I, and our
short meeting was fraught with peril. Such business was never protracted with
social amenities. In his note to me he asked obliquely for contributions to what*

was by then more than a cabinet—cases, most likely—of natural objects, saying only that any specimens unwanted, unused, unshipped, unspoken for might find a welcome home. I should have traveled to him in Manhattan, should have been generous, for Samuel told me he was one of the few men of science who encouraged and worked with women. Indeed, in one volume of the Transactions, he thanked Miss Lizzie Williams, who, though a teacher of art, collected an herbarium of Kansas plants with Mudge at the college. She left the state before I could meet her. I did have correspondence with Mrs. Wells, of the entomology collection, who worked exhaustively for Mudge and science.

Perhaps I will make a visit, say Decoration Day, to pay my respects to Mrs. Mudge, to visit the cemetery—surely there will soon be an impressive monument of some sort erected there—and to see the cabinet, likely his finest memorial.

Letter to Sally Miller

Thursday, October 14, 1880
Lawrence, KS

Dear Sally—

Sometimes I must admit envy. You, your butterflies, your husband having
learned to respect your passion for collecting, and who now helps you in the
task of finding, crating, and shipping your specimens. The beauty of your
specimens. Perhaps I should have studied prairie flowers, with their colorful
blossoms, their deep roots, their ability to thrive our sunstruck summers, our
bitter winters, our late and early frosts, our droughts, our fires, hailstorms,
and cyclones.

Plants are bred, and so I suppose we feel they are harmless. Butterflies
flutter airy and light—they are winged magic. We do not notice them
breeding, but we are fascinated by eggs, larvae, cocoons, the entire cycle of
their lives.

Fossils breed mystery, suspicion, even fear. For what are they? Certainly
they are not beautiful, nor of value, like gems. They hint at an unimaginable
world, a world thus unimagined but by the few of us who seek to solve their
mystery. My penchant for them, my love for my bryozoans, is barely tolerated here by the many. I think the very existence of fossils, and someone
interested in them, creates fear, for the fossil record leads to questions: of
time, of the long evolution of the earth, of the classification of eons, eras
with names as difficult to pronounce as the fossils themselves. Yet I love
each heretical syllable—Quaternary, Paleogene, Cretaceous, Silurian, Ordo-
vician, Proterozoic, to name a few.

Sally, I hope to hear news of any discoveries you make. I am not certain I will understand how you discern traits and characteristics that might change the classification of genus and species, as you outlined in your last letter, but the same is happening in the fossil world, in all the world of science, as we live in a time of mystery, discovery, hypothesis, and theory.

I often think of you, traversing your countryside with butterfly net in hand, alert and untiring in your pursuit of what you've never seen before. I do the same, my eye on the world for something so unique and original that it will change the world, or at least our understanding of it.

Like you, I do not seek to change the behavior of the world—though I once did try, like Hugh Cameron, with his steamings. Kansas was to change the world, but it remains too much the same in its human terms. I do not wish to build and grow the world, like the bankers and railroad men with whom I am forced to do business. I do not wish to educate or preach toward any kind of salvation or enlightenment. Instead, I simply want to see clearly, to find the world. Do you feel this way, too?

Let me know. Please name a time when I might journey to you again, or you to me. I would cherish even a few brief moments of your company.

Sincerely, Nell

Letter from Sally Miller

Dear Nell—

I am sorry for my delay in writing to you. I had hoped that I could invite
you to come for a visit, but that is not to be. Some hard times have hit us,
and I can hardly bear to write it down. We had a fire, a bad one, and in it I
lost all of my butterflies. Years of collecting are now nothing but ash. As
Horace says, we can replace boards, we can buy more furniture, we can
rebuild our house, but we cannot make my collection what it was, ever
again. I can only thank God for each specimen I shipped away, sometimes
with regret that I might never see it again. I could not rebuild my collection
for years, and even then I don't think I will ever find some of the rare specimens that I was lucky enough to trap when they wandered into my sphere.

Your letters to me—they are now ash, too, so I have only my memory
to rely on. How I hope you have saved drafts of them, as you told me you
often do, so maybe someday I will see them. I have lost so much. You were
jealous of my butterflies, because of their beauty and because people
understand them and maybe understand me, also, when I want so much to
collect them. Now it is my turn to be jealous of you and your stones.
Stones don't burn. Yes, you collect dead things, but dead things fossilized
in rock do not perish.

I think that I might well come to you for a visit. Horace is so busy with
rebuilding. He is, as I said, distraught about our loss, but I fear he cannot
truly understand it. I leave the hotel where we live now, and find one of my
meditations, and spend an hour in the company of my thoughts. Each time

I think I will resolve my grief, or make a plan, or find an opportunity in my loss, like maybe forgetting butterflies and beginning to collect moths, those dusty and drab cousins of butterflies, or perhaps just collect one kind of butterfly, or do an experiment charting the growth of butterflies from the time they emerge from their cocoons to the time they die—how much do they change size, weight, coloration? I don't know. Each time I come back from a meditation, Horace eyes me almost suspiciously, hoping that I've put my grief behind me, that I will be an attentive helpmate and partner in the rebuilding that lies ahead. So far, his hope has not been rewarded, for I return as befuddled and heartbroken as when I left. Travel might invigorate me, my friend Nell, if you have room and time for a lost soul.

Horace has already given me permission to do as I please in this. He is bent on rebuilding, and that will help him replace his sense of what we have lost. He will replace the house. He will not listen to my fears, which I hate to even write down in this letter to you, but I feel I must. What if someone started the fire that burned our home? Was it just the wayward coal popping from the fireplace onto the carpet as Horace believes, or did someone enter and cause this havoc? You know that our politics, our very lives, are different from the Missourians around us. You know that Horace has stirred opinion with his free thinking. I have told him that perhaps he is more Kansan than Missourian, but he was born here, and he will stay here in spite of differences with his neighbors. I shudder to think that it was one of those neighbors who ordered me off of his land recently when I was on a butterfly outing, or one of those who voted against Horace in his last attempt to become mayor, or one of those Horace beat in his recent legal case against the people who wanted to take Andrews's land for an expansion of the railroad depot. You know what it is like to have people look at you askance, and since the fire, I feel exposed, examined, as pinned by public opinion as one of my butterflies to the specimen card. Why does everyone blame rather than sympathize? I overheard one person mutter about the chemicals I use—the chloroform and formaldehyde—that surely fed the fire.

Horace thinks me silly. He tells me my mind is flitting to and fro like one of my butterflies, and maybe he is right. I feel flighty, blown about by winds of disappointment and change, for where now is my purpose? Do we simply start all over and rebuild as Horace wishes? These things are hard to settle in my mind, Nell, and so Horace approves a trip to you, to Lawrence, where I might have sympathetic company and heal the scars of our fire.

Please write to me soon, in care of the Liberty Hotel, with word about whether I would be welcome there. I have imagined myself striding your prairie, helping you in your work, seeing what you see and how you see it. This would be better than what I see whenever I close my eyes: my house smoldering, smoke rising from still burning embers.

Your friend,
Sally

Letter to Sally Miller

Tuesday, May 17, 1881
Lawrence, KS

Dear Sally—

Come as soon as you can, poor thing. I was rescued from the fire that
burned down my father and mother's cabin at a ferry station across the
Hatchie River in Tennessee in 1825. I saw the flames of the Free State Hotel,
set afire by the ugly brigand Samuel Jones in 1856. My porch was set on fire
during Quantrill's Raid on Lawrence in 1863, my Solomon brutally murdered. Yes, stone saved me then, and, I suppose, continues to save me. Like
Lawrence, I have been forced to be phoenix. Fly to me, Sally, and stay as
long as you'd like. I will take you to those places that calm me. Together, we
will hope and plan and restore you to yourself.

Send a telegram when you leave the station, and I will be waiting, dear
friend.

Yours,
Nell

Diary Entry

Sally Miller. Warmth and breath. I had forgotten just how alone, though not lonely, I have become. With Sally at my side, her soft exhalations of breath, her occasional flutterings that cannot quite be named snoring, her flow of words as we wake, dress, lay the kettle on for tea, I feel comforted.

Solomon and I had just such a domestic life. I did not think to experience such ease ever again, at least not away from my family in Arkansas. What a friend I have found in Sally. This day she parts, returning to the home Horace has built for them. She flies to him eagerly, as they share similar comfort between them. I will miss her warmth. Two embers together can produce four times the heat. Even Sally's words of wonder and encouragement are like a fanning of a hot coal.

Sally returns to comfort, but not to work. She will not begin anew her collection of butterflies. "A time of my life that is over," she said, as she has come to understand herself. As a young woman she read novels, those guides to life, those lessons to learn, that empathy to share, those wonderful characters to love—the Emmas and Mollys, Janes and Elizabeths. Then she put them aside for the natural world, and her lepidoptera. "I go home to discover what might be next," she says.

I wish her well. I have had too many nexts forced upon me to give up my bryozoans. I shall die, and stones and rocks will mark me. Sally has encouraged me in my study. She was going to write, to share her knowledge with the world. Now she cannot, her specimens all lost. So I must do as she would. "Your fossils cannot be lost, stones as they are. Help them speak."

In Sally's honor, I will take her suggestion.

Diary Entry

For my entertainment tonight I have braved terrible cold to see a theatrical piece showing at the Bowersock Opera House. The playbills called The Maid of Arran *a drama that would "ensnare all hearts," that would "leave an impress of beauty and nobility within the sordid mind of man." Well, this woman was not much ensnared by the Irish drama, sentimental, overlong, with a shouting quartet of players. Miss Genevieve Rogers and Miss Agnes Hallack were quite lovely, as actresses are expected to be. They were no doubt drained by their tour, from New York, through Chicago, it was said, for they were pale and seemed to flee the stage for rest at each opportunity. Frank Aiken was as good as his reputation. The young actor who also wrote the drama, a Mr. Lyman Frank Baum, exaggerated his movements as much as his play exaggerated the exigencies of romance. I wonder if he will find any success, for though his dialogue showed wit, his plotting of the events had all the surprise of a thrice-told joke.*

All amusement was frozen by the temperature, I suppose. I longed not for better theater, I suppose, but for better climate; I would have been more tolerant of small flaws had I seen this same drama as a matinee on a sunlit day, with unwilted flowers on the stage, with fresh faces from the players, with an audience that did not stamp feet to encourage circulation to the toes. I braved the cold but remained chilled, and so I write, perhaps unfairly, about this troupe who certainly have ambitions beyond the small towns of Kansas.

Letter to Sally Miller

My dear Sally—

Yes to all you have said. I am happy to hear that your husband has agreed to support you in this cause, for if anyone might be able to persuade women and men alike, it would be you, who has such a fine balance of logic and warmth. Your particular argument is the better one. The focus on inequality has merit, and yet many interpret the stridency of unfairness as a negative. That black men, former slaves, many of them poorly educated, can vote, while women cannot, is indeed unjust. Equally unjust is the assumption that women as a class are "better" than those men empowered with suffrage by the 15th Amendment.

Much better is your argument that this nation needs women as voters, for it focuses on the strengths of women as people who nurture, people who care for the hearth and the heart, people with a keen sense of justice, people contributing everywhere in churches, schools, and politics, too, though behind the main stage. What can be said against infusing the voting populace with the best of what women might offer?

I read the speech you enclosed in your letter with great interest, and can see you at the hustings, your curls escaping one of your massive hats, your eyes afire, your voice loud enough to be heard by a crowd, yet delivering your message with the calm reassurances of its arguments. I wish you well. Only one note. I caution against the overuse of the word "domestic," along with the phrase "domestic sphere." We were never "wild," so let us not be "domesticated." I suggest inserting the words home and hearth, which is where so many women show their capabilities—though I confess I am not among them.

I also suggest that you might have a more ready audience for your words in Kansas, reformers as we are known to be. Women worked their magic through the WCTU, and we have prohibition and active women's clubs working toward the same next step you desire for women everywhere.

Write to me soon. I must know how you are received in your new venture. Please take comfort that you represent me in your fight to bring the vote to women.

Your loving friend,
Nell

Diary Entry

My widowhood has reached its majority—twenty-one years without you, my Solomon. When we married at twenty-three, I thought myself old. Now, at fifty-nine, I realize that the twenty-three years before we married, and the twenty-one years after your death make the mere fifteen years we had together seem even shorter. Courtship—the wooden ring you carved. Wedding—the gold ring you exchanged for the wooden one, the night golden, too. The loss of Benjamin—a hole in the damp soil filled with relentless tears, then earth. The loss of Lawrence—even while you were in Lawrence, returning as you did to a mound of earth instead of the flesh we'd hoped for. The move to Lawrence—with my grief an extra burden, I know it. Our fifteen years seems but a moment.

Solomon, you were my love, my companion, my protection, my salvation. Now, with the passing of years, I have learned to be my own companion, protection, and salvation. Widows never stop grieving, but widows are also singular people, not people suddenly halved, never to be whole again. I regret your death, and will regret it all of my life. Had you not been brutally taken from me, I might never have pursued my scientific interests, but as each day passes I think of how, were you living, I would share my thoughts, my adventures, my discoveries, my studies along with my love for you. Solomon, you would have been the kind of husband who encouraged me, as I encouraged you, each of us taking a part in the other's life, two wills bent together toward doing what was right. We were crusaders, and you would have understood my crusade in a way others might not.

Were we not raised in the same countryside? Did we not venture into the natural world every chance we could? Did we not remove rocks from caves so dark we could not see, but could only feel, that they were edged in crystals that would gleam in the sun? Did we not want everything to be revealed, to be seen, to be understood by light of day? Oh, Solomon, I lost in you a kindred spirit. In being the spirited woman I am, I honor you. I reach my majority, twenty-one years as widow, and I honor you still.

Sketch of Nell Johnson Doerr.

Letter to Sister Mary

Wednesday, June 10, 1885
Lawrence, KS

Dear Mary—

He had not meant to be impertinent, but, of course, he was. Youngish—I cannot judge the age of young men any longer, not having had a son. With that smug sneer of the partially educated, he fairly burst into the museum, demanding to see Dr. Willcott. "For all the news of these fresh discoveries of the ancient," he said. At my age, Mary, I am the ancient discoverer of freshness. So many are so particularly, even willfully, naïve about fossils and their meaning. I accompanied Willcott to the young man's side.

Dr. Willcott received him well, of course. He believes in public education, since he works with students at a state university. Down we went into the laboratory. Willcott pulled drawer after drawer containing recent discoveries, some of them my own, of fossil bryozoans. He explained these tiny creatures, how their single cells communicate with others, how they join together, how some of them function as filters, others as locomotors, others as digesters of ocean nutrients.

"Ocean?" the young man asked, bewildered, for we had told him that all the bryozoan collection had been found in the Pennsylvanian rock of eastern Kansas.

"Ocean, yes. The ocean of Kansas," said Willcott. "We live atop a world we can only imagine."

The young man wrote something in his thin notebook. He examined the content of the several drawers. "I see lines. Am I to see lines?" he asked.

"You see the fossilized remains of ancient bryozoans, yes, each part once whole." Dr. Willcott went to the cabinet and opened a door. Inside was the one complete bryozoan I'd found in my years of collecting. Like a fan, like braided hair, like the tassel of a curtain, intricate and beautiful—Oh, Mary, you've seen my drawings.

"May I?" asked the journalist, though he had already grasped the specimen. Willcott tried to intercept his hand, and in a sickening jostle the specimen dropped to the terrazzo floor.

Mary, I nearly fainted. The young man saw it in my face, and reached for my arm to hold me up. I found a chair and sat. The young man bent to his knees and began to piece together what was now nothing but litter. "You have a chance to study our fresh discoveries," said Willcott. He took my hand, and we climbed the stairs, leaving the young man to try to make sense of the chaos of what once thrived on the ocean floor. Unlike us, Mary, he would never see it as anything but ancient ruins.

You know what I've been doing all day today, I'm sure. I will find another complete bryozoan. I must. Write to me soon.

Your loving sister,
Nell

Diary Entry

I always come to knowledge with regret. I am happy to discover a new way of thinking and knowing, but regret lingers in this *thought: had I known earlier, how much better would my work have been. I stumbled upon fossils like a child, unaware but fascinated. I picked them up and carried them to my home, soon forgetting exactly where I'd found each one, thus rendering them less useful to science.*

Then I learned to log discoveries, note weather conditions, place, companion plants, time of day, everything I could observe. Then I learned to measure and chart height on bluff, and kind of rock. I did that so simply, Permian/Pennsylvanian. Now we know more. We have refined our stratum, we have stratigrified. We have made uniform the species and subspecies names of what I often labeled "bryozoan?" and I feel the fool, the Eve who suddenly realizes, with knowledge, that she is naked in the Garden. I wish to hide my ignorance as she hid her nakedness, but there it is, on display, all the drawings and labels and information scrawled on paper, looking like the handwriting of a child rather than the considered work of an adult.

Are we all children in this pursuit we call science? Will all of our work seem childish to future generations who have come to more and better knowledge, more and better classifications, more ways to study rocks using new means—stronger chemicals and microscopes and other means I cannot even imagine? Perhaps everyone who practices in the sciences should welcome being made to look foolish, for that means progress has been made. We stand on what we think is the topmost rung of the ladder, yet the ladder is always being extended by knowledge. We feel we have climbed leagues, and yet the ladder is of infinite, and therefore unimaginable, height. We feel dizzy at the top of the ladder—so much to know, so much to find out, so much hypothesis—and yet future generations will see what a short way we managed to climb in our short time of discovery.

Would that we could see the entire ladder, the entire scope of what we are capable of coming to know. The thought alone excites me.

Notes

Begin by thanking the men who have taken time to educate me in science (Winston, Mudge, Forster, now Willcott), and those who have learned not to be threatened by my interests (Whitaker, Watson, Woodhouse, Jenkins, Littlefield). Mention the support of Cameron?

Thank the Academy for its interest in Permian/Pennsylvanian fossils, bryozoans in particular. Note the many fascinating presentations published in the *Transactions* by men (Mudge, Williston, Savage), and the helpful exploration of science that the publication represents. Note, too, that they focus largely on vertebrate fossils, which the Western part of the state has in abundance.

Make note of the progress made in Kansas over the past twenty years, from the classification of types of rocks matched with periods—Permian, Pennsylvanian, Cretaceous—with the discovery of excellent sites among our quarries and rail lines. As we build the state for commerce and education, we reveal the geologic and biologic past on which we stand. Note the current robustness of geological studies, and the Kansas contribution to national knowledge. Note the creation of reputation among our scientists. (Men love compliments even more than women.)

Explain my own interest in the invertebrate (find the talk given to the Unitarian women—though largely unscientific, it makes a case for colonizing invertebrates, their tenaciousness, their adaptability, their many and fascinating forms, which will lead into my further notes on variety).

Begin to note the variety of bryozoans found in Douglas County on the sandbars, along the river bluffs, and in the railroad cutaways. In four specific locations, I have found over twenty-seven different kinds of bryozoan life forms. Name those for the assemblage, with adequate descriptions.

Ask, rather than assert, two different positions. 1. Does this variety show that the warm and shallow seabed of Kansas was at one single time teeming with evolutionary possibilities for the shaping of many different forms, and manifesting them in such variety all at once? Or, 2. Does this variety show that in the same location, but at different evolutionary times, depending on conditions, some bryozoan forms flourished, then died away as conditions changed, and sometime later others formed differently, layering themselves, but in such shallow layers, that they seem to all have been alive at the same time, when they might be separated by as much as centuries?

End by saying that these questions may not be possible to answer at the current time, but assert—go ahead at least a little—that perhaps, if the answer to these inquiries is indeed important, that all of us should pay more and closer attention to what invertebrates can tell us. After all, the large-boned vertebrates are unique to time and place, living and thriving in an ocean that is no more. Bryozoans are still living, all over the globe, and their study—especially comparing contemporary with fossil forms—might be able to tell us more about evolutionary tendencies than the study of all those exciting creatures with teeth, as exotic and distinct as they are. End in a demure fashion, for though I would like to assert, I am not a professional geologist or paleontologist—only a curious amateur. While conceding that, I might position myself better by again thanking the many men whose work has taught me and inspired me. Would that they would be in the audience.

Be certain to attend as many sessions as possible, and fill up with science. Even if it is just Snow and his bird lists, again, remember that he is as interested in them and their variety as I am in bryozoans.

Diary Entry

I am emboldened by the keynote address given at the beginning of our Emporia gathering by Dr. John C. Branner, University of Indiana. He titled it, "Geologists, Professional and Unprofessional." I know which of those categories names me, and yet his assertion that the unprofessional has a role in science is comforting. Of course he is correct that bad science is worse than no science, for it clouds the very water we are trying to see through toward truth. But he defines unprofessional differently than I expected. For him, the unprofessional is not someone unpedigreed, someone unattached to a university or other institution, someone amateur like myself. Instead, unprofessional is to be defined in terms of behavior, in terms of slipshod work, in terms of those who collect without detail, uprooting rocks, minerals, and fossils from their resting place without documenting time and place, and thus forever disconnecting a specimen from useful context, rendering it thereby unfit to add to our knowledge of science.

He likened it to those people who might take fossil teeth and make a necklace out of them, to wear like savages, without ever trying to understand why the tooth of a shark might be found in Kansas, or some other place. Instead, an important fossil find dangles around a primitive neck, weighing down a head instead of enlightening it. "We know so much more than we did thirty years ago," Dr. Branner said, "and yet we could know so much more were we all to act professionally. All of us, no matter our education, must become educators, ambassadors for science, must articulate the best practice of science and the proper methods of collecting. We must engage everything—animal, vegetable, mineral—in such a way that it can add to, rather than detract from, our understanding of the natural world."

I hoped while I listened to John Branner that he might attend my humble presentation, but I did not think he would. I was surprised when he slipped into the back of the room midway through. After, he shook my hand. He complimented me as someone who was "meticulously professional in my collection records."

"You are a collector, mostly, is that correct?" he asked. He eyed me as though I were a specimen of some kind, folding his arms across his chest.

I agreed that I was.

"But you have asked questions this weekend?" His tone was almost accusing.

"Yes," I admitted.

"Good," he said. He suddenly clapped his hands. "You are climbing the ladder of science."

"I hope so," I said, "as I hope all of us are." I almost spoke of my own sense of science as an infinite ladder, all of us climbing to the top.

But he had more to say, and he took my hand in his. "Science has methodology, my dear woman, as I'm sure you know. You gather data with accurate observation, using the human eye, and measurements, and you record. You classify and organize your data. All of this you have done. You have gathered, but what do these gatherings say to you? What speaks the stone? With your delivery here you are asking your specimens to speak. You have moved to the next step. You have generalized, you have begun to formulate questions, perhaps even hinted at a theory."

"I am unsure of my speculations," I admitted.

"As are each of us," he said. "Science demands we make theories so that we might test them. Nell Doerr, I entreat you to test them. Science is not complete until you verify theory with more data. And until you report on your findings for verification or criticism. I hope you will accomplish those next rungs on the ladder, for you have proven capable in everything you have done up to this point."

I nodded my head, hardly able to look Dr. Branner in the eye.

"I entreat you," he said again, and smiled.

He shook my hand once more. I fear I blushed. I fear I am still blushing with his confidence in me, his exhortation still lingering.

Letter from Sally Miller

Friday, April 15, 1887
Waverly, MO

Dearest Nell—

I must thank you for your generous hospitality these last several months.
Would that I could stay with you longer, but my work in Kansas has been
brought to fruition—I still pinch myself that municipal suffrage for women
has passed, and Susanna Madora Salter of Argonia, Kansas, has become the
first woman mayor in the United States. There is more to come, surely, and I
will be on the front lines here in Missouri, and everywhere I am invited to
speak for the rights of women.

Horace has difficulty with my being gone for long stretches of time.
He was jealous, too, of my butterflies, at first, then he joined with me. I
have asked for the same with suffrage, but he has yet to agree. I believe he
tolerates my trips, my campaigning, my "speechifying," as he calls it, only
because I am supported financially by those people who wish for a better
future for women. Each time I return home, I fear that he may have taken
to the bottle for solace, but I see no sign of it. He reassures me, saying, "A
healed scar makes for tougher skin, and reminds you always of the
wound." Thankfully, he will not wound himself, nor our marriage, again.
Of course, I'd prefer his support, but like so many men he will tolerate
the change he foresees happening but will not work to help make the
change.

You, of course, have always been active in your causes, whether abolition
or science. You have joined me as a suffragist, too, but you are, in your spirit,

more an activist, if there is such a word.[*] You spoke to me of giving more voice to your science. The vote is giving voice, too. What we do helps both of us. All of your support has helped me become what I have. Do you remember when I felt the need for my meditations? Always alone, always hoping, always wishing. Now my meditations, like yours, are put to paper, are spoken aloud. Thank you for your encouragement.

Thank you for your love!

I am yours,
Sally Miller

---

[*] In actuality, there was not a word—the first known usage appeared between 1905–1915. Still, Sally Miller is prescient in her coinage.

Diary Entry

To find a trove late in the day! A curse, a hurried curse, for in October, the mortality of the day is sudden with shadows, and I am reminded of just how much I work against time. I have so little of that precious commodity, and so much to discover. As dusk obscures rock, silhouettes trees, and dulls the eye at the end of the day, it also darkens my patience.

Perhaps each dusk simply reminds me of all I have yet to do. Perhaps what I thought was a trove is simply all that will forever be hidden from me, and my yearning for it excites my sense that it is just about to be unearthed, yet is just beyond my grasp. When I return to the quarry at first light, will I find all that seemed possible at dusk? Will it be within reach, or will daylight reveal my impatience, rendering me to the obligation of another day of patient searching?

When I was a young girl, time seemed expansive, each day set before me as a gift. I spent equal time at work and play, most often unhurried. I had no obligations that urged me beyond their physical and mental challenge. I might wash dishes after a supper that included guests. I might climb a tree. I might find where Craney, our wayward laying hen, was hiding her eggs this time—I was always the one to find them before they rotted. I might read a book, or conjugate Latin verbs, or write a short interpretation of a Biblical parable. All with seeming patience. Now, urgency eggs me toward impatience, dissatisfaction, with the sense that I may never achieve much at all.

What do you need to achieve, Nell Johnson Doerr? Admit to it—the complete moss bryozoan to replace the one shattered? A bryozoan not yet studied? A discovery in a location, or a kind of rock, not expected to support a population of bryozoans? What would satisfy impatience? Perhaps all or nothing. Perhaps impatience is but a stumbling through darkness after dusk turns to moonless night that makes us aware of ourselves—that we are nothing more nor less than any other creature, vulnerable and struggling blindly for home, each day a kind of triumph, each day a kind of failure.

Letter from J. L. Smith

Monday, September 24, 1888
National Museum, Washington, DC

Dear Nell Doerr—

I took a lesson from your first correspondence to me and made certain your paper was considered under the authorship of N. J. Doerr, and did not reveal that I knew you until after the decision was made. And the decision has been made. You are to present, here in Washington, on your theory of bryozoan evolution and its potential to tell the scientific community about the evolutionary conditions of the great inland sea, its condition and environment, its temperature and fluxuations, its waxings and wanings. You have moved beyond collector—you know how much I respect your skills in that area—and have put forth a theory that will have many in the invertebrate community looking afresh at their specimens, and at your own that you have sent here for so many years.

Of course, after your paper was accepted for presentation, I revealed my connection to you. At this time, those in the Academy are discussing whether, now that they know your sex, to allow you to address them. This has never been done before. I told them if they accepted the paper without the prejudice of sex, then they should allow the woman who wrote the paper to speak to them, unsullied by prejudice. I will write soon of their decision, for I have already said that you should at least be allowed to attend our annual meeting.

I could not wait to write with the news of acceptance, though, and be sure that all will be arranged. We will pay for your travel, and you will be housed and dined at our expense. This is the least we can do for someone who has had such a long and mutually profitable relationship with the National Museum. In the meantime, if you will continue to ready your presentation—larger drawings would be appropriate, and some we can publish for distribution.

Mrs. Smith is looking forward to meeting you, as am I, of course, though I feel I know you through the correspondence we've shared over the years. Others are eager to meet you as well, and, since you have never been to the nation's capital, we will make sure that you have time for sightseeing and cultural events while you are here. Mrs. Smith wishes to know if you would like to attend the opera, as Dr. Richard Jones, of Princeton University, and his wife, Maise, are particularly fond, and always attend when they are here. We will make certain you come to know them as well.

I hope to have more news soon. In the meanwhile let us prepare for January, and the national meeting. Again, my congratulations.

Sincerely,
Dr. J. L. Smith

Diary Entry

Are these drawings sufficient for such an audience? I have found complete Praso-pora to add to my evidence that many bryozoans occupy the same space—but at what time or times, and how can we know? Surely they were separate evolutions over a long time, as conditions on the planet changed. Being sensitive, and deli-cate, bryozoans might have evolved, then died out, thousands of times over a long period of time. And so it could be that each fossil I find, each fossil I hold in my hand, could come from a different decade, century, even millennia. I will draw and draw, but still be unable to render my discoveries and my thoughts clearly. Such is the way of the world, perhaps. We are ever in the dark, and we must braille toward understanding.*

---

* Although I cannot be certain the figure included here is the one Nell is referencing, as Nell Doerr's valise contains many drawings, it is one of a Prasopora. Nell might well have given her best drawings to the National Museum, since they also collected her fossils. We may never know when she showed the most capability in her drawings.

Diary Entry

I am on a train, riding toward humiliation. Honor came when my little paper was accepted by the National Academy. N. J. Doerr was the author, whose work, "mostly a catalogue by an amateur paleontologist, dedicated to invertebrate fossils in the Midwest, but a rather useful catalogue for its variety," was deemed worthy of presentation. Dr. Smith wrote, too, that "the speculations about the survival of some species and the extinctions of others, as well as the variety of bryozoan fossils found in the same place, will prove a worthy topic for discussion."

"Not, however, if discussed by a woman." He was my advocate, but when the Academy discovered me to be Nell Johnson Doerr, a widow living in Lawrence, Kansas, the invitation to read was first withdrawn in favor of an agreement to publish my paper in the annual Notes. *Smith negotiated an amelioration, suggesting that his professor and mentor Dr. Richard Jones, of Princeton University, be allowed to read my paper in my stead.*

With a firm hand I held the train ticket from Lawrence to Washington, DC. No woman, I was told, had ever been allowed in the audience during National Academy proceedings except for the British paleontologist Mary Anning, who had discovered the great mosasaurs, buttressing Darwin's theories. She was forced to sit in a chair in the back of the room, boothed, behind a draping curtain so that she might hear but not be seen.

They will no doubt do the same to me. I will be allowed to hear my words. I will have the satisfaction of my own presence. I will make them aware of me, though all they will see is a curtain. Remember, for centuries men stared, oblivious, at the fossils in rocks. They did so with little curiosity, with little investigation. They curtained their minds with fear, unable to question creation. Behind the veil of my curtain, I will be what they refuse to see, fearful of my authority and of any change in social custom. I will be patient, waiting for discovery, waiting to be taken seriously, one of many women—my own Sally Miller, among them—who are eager to participate fully in the educational, political, scientific life of this nation.

Letter to Sister Mary

Tuesday, January 29, 1889
Washington, DC

Dearest Mary—

In Arkansas we more often made music than listened to it—Father with
his fiddle, Mama with her spoons. In church we sang hymns. Yes, at
dances and fairs and town picnics we were entertained, but by people like
ourselves; nobody was professional. Nor were we dressed in any extraordi-
nary way. Always we have been unaccustomed to costume. So imagine me,
Mary, in a splendid dress, in our nation's capital, at the National Theatre.
As I wrote you earlier, my paper was read to the National Academy by
Dr. Richard Jones, of Princeton University—as no woman had taken the
podium at their august meeting, and no woman was likely to interrupt
that tradition. After the reading, and a brief discussion of my paper,
well-received as it was, I was escorted from my curtained enclosure and
taken to the hotel where Dr. Richard Jones and his lovely wife had
secured rooms.

"A special treat," said Maise. "We'll take dinner, then attend opera."

Mary, with but a light knock on my door, Maise entered my room with
finery I've never imagined. "We are the same size, I notice, and I won't wear
this dress during our excursion anyway." Dress, yes, but matching hat,
gloves, shoes, all silver and flowing, as though I were to become a walking
fountain of bubbling, nearly incandescent water. She insisted on a slight bit
of powder and rouge; she defined my lips; she combed my hair, and tied it
up so that the hat might crown me. "Like a princess," she said. I am much
too old, at sixty-four, to think of myself as a princess, and much too humble

to be a queen, but Maise was certainly my fairy godmother, transporting me into splendor I had never witnessed before.

At the theater a box was reserved for the Joneses, and for a colleague of Richard's, Dr. Gilbert, who escorted me. We heard a set of operatic arias by the National Company, accompanied by a fine orchestra. Mary, the curtain opened to women on the stage. They nodded to the male conductor and directed *him* to begin. Their voices, soprano and alto, brought Mozart and Rossini, Beethoven, Offenbach, and Verdi to us, resounding with a power that still thrills me, though several days have passed. I not only heard opera for the first time, I heard WOMEN. I heard the female voice, unencumbered, unselfconscious, unabashed, *unleashed*.

In these beautiful arias there was triumph and command. There was joy and laughter. And there was great sadness. They performed Verdi's "Willow Song" with its "Ave Maria," which premiered only last year in New York, and a more melancholy piece has yet to beset me. As Desdemona sings, she foretells her own death at the hands of Otello. Verdi captures her completely. She leaps from the lowest to the highest registers. She is vulnerable, resigned, wronged, and yet accepting. Her strength inspired me to tears. I went home with opera in my head. As I undressed I came back into my own body, my own striving self, an old woman who has known beauty but is not beautiful, who knows science but is not quite a scientist, who has a voice but does not quite sing. Still I am content with this day. If not great myself, I have sat in the presence of greatness—of science and of music.

Will I ever hear such music again? Will I ever be able to compose another acceptable paper? All night in my dreams I sang the assertions of my article on a stage, my science as powerful as an aria, as trained and beautiful as opera.

Dare I assert that science will soon join the arts in expressing the beauty and joy of humanity and its place in the natural world? Dare I say that women will help to make this possible? Not soon, of course. But, Mary, you must remember I am trained to think beyond months and years, rather in millennia, eons, and ages. I see us uncurtained.

Your loving sister,
Nell

Letter from Brother Hiram and Sister Mary

Wednesday, June 12, 1889
Pine Bluff, AR

Dearest Sister—

All of us here in Arkansas have been thrilled by your adventures in Washington, DC. What an honor to have your ideas presented to a national academy. Did you ever expect such a thing? I did. From the first time you wrote me about your fossils, you were very exact and determined. You always were stubborn. I had a letter from Jacob. You know he's continuing his studies at Oberlin College. In Science. Geology. Where did he get that idea? Do you remember your first visit, how he held that little archimedes in his hand and wouldn't let go? Thank you for introducing him to that world. What a world. You push forward by studying things from the long-ago past. Anyway, Mary is eager to add to this letter, so I will say good-bye.

Your loving brother, Hiram

Dear Nell—

I can only echo what Hiram has written you about our pride in you. You are a model for all of us, particularly we women. I won't call you stubborn, but I agree with "determined." Persistent, too. Not everyone can see what others cannot see. Not everyone can keep learning against custom. Not everyone can continue to make discoveries and send them to collectors to study and classify. You have unearthed a new world.

I understand women received the right to vote in Kansas, your dear friend Sally Miller helping in the cause, and I wonder how it might feel to go to a polling place and cast a ballot based on my own judgement. To be thought worthy and intelligent enough to change the course of political life. We women, with all our best qualities, will someday be recognized as vital to the national life of our government. Who, after all, has better governed children, men, and themselves? Here in Arkansas we hear much talk of women's suffrage, but we have yet to secure it, and I fear it will be years—so many that I will not live to see it.

In Kansas you have unearthed new worlds. All those years ago, when you left with Solomon, I could only mourn our loss of you. But what a difference Kansas made in the fight against slavery. Though that terrible struggle took your Solomon, you persisted, and Kansas persisted. Prohibition and suffrage, and what next? You have also unearthed the importance of science. You have also unearthed yourself. I imagine you in Washington, hearing your words read from a lectern. You may have been behind a curtain, certainly, but, like a fossil discovery, you are about to be seen and heard and understood. Nell, you have found much, including yourself. Forgive me for ever questioning you—your marriage to Solomon, your move to Lawrence, your persistence with fossils, your forthrightness for women. I have come to understand these matters more of late, as I grow older, and my children show me how to live in a new world. They anticipate a new century with eagerness; I simply hope to live so long.

May this letter of congratulations, echoed from all the voices in your family, find you well, and satisfied with yourself.

Your loving sister, Mary

Shoes found in Nell's valise, likely her own from her youth and her adulthood.

Letter to Jacob Johnson

Thursday, August 15, 1889
Lawrence, KS

My dear Nephew—

How happy I am to learn of your interest in geology. We have so much to discover, to learn, to understand, to make sense of. The study of our earth and its layers will give us the keys to the understanding of our origins, from a time in the past seemingly eternal in length, to now, to what stretches before us—or not strictly us, but the matter from which we are formed.

Your father reminded me in a letter of your very early attraction to fossils, your delight at nine months with a bryozoan archimedes, which I believe you still possess today. I am so very proud of you, and this letter proposes to tell you that, for the young are often not praised at the outset of their careers. I praise you, as I was not always praised at the beginning of my pursuits. I support you, as I was not always supported at the earliest moments that I was willing to share my discoveries. I applaud the work you will do, the papers you will write, the differences you will make to geology. I do this when you need it most—when you have yet to accomplish what I know you will accomplish. Encouragement is necessary, for you will need courage. Science is often viewed as suspect, even near the end of this century, for people too often see it as in opposition to religion and belief. Never argue a false dichotomy. Science loves the word "and" more than the word "versus." I know you will do well in your studies.

This letter also proposes to explain the gift you have no doubt discovered in this package. The watch belonged to Solomon Doerr, killed by Quantrill in Kansas Territory four years before you were born, given to him by his father, Sherwood Doerr. Though many years old now, the watch has never kept but perfect time. I have used it these many years (except for a brief period during which it was lost) to help me in the logging of my fossil discoveries. The watch has been my companion, and a fine one it is. You will be studying time. A watch tracks the temporal, but with each tick, had it a memory, it would be moving deeper into and away from time itself. You will study that, and come to know, as I have, the grinding slowness of geologic time, and the rapid ticktocking of the all-too-ephemeral present.

Let this watch be a companion to you. Let it remind you of your Uncle Solomon, whose time was too short. Let it remind you of me, who loves you, and takes such pride in you. Let it remind you of family, of connections, of time itself in all its machinations. Bless you as you begin your studies. I hope to be able to visit with you soon.

Your loving aunt,
Nell

Letter to Mother Jo

My dearest Mother Jo—

This is a letter of thanks. Although you know what I will say, I need to write this down, for neither of us can stop the passage of time, and too many miles separate us. Our intimacies have been fewer than either of us would have wished, yet I ever feel the closeness we share when we are together.

Yes, we are together, always, no matter the physical distance. My first memories still stand forth every day, to be counted for the gifts they are. I remember learning my letters, as you did, night after night with the alphabet—you called them "A, B, Z's"—then putting letters together into words—you called them "A, An, and The's"—and reading from the Bible—the "begats"—and going to spelling bees even before I was in school. Your fierce intensity for learning started the reading and formation of sentences but moved so quickly into the forming of paragraphs, thoughts, ideas. "We are born to learn," you told me again and again, and you have continued to learn, and to teach me to learn, throughout our lives. Your hunger for everything—mathematics, geography, and history, for Latin, philosophy, and geology, for religions, literature, and science—and your desire to learn it as I learned it, taught me that anyone can learn anything and at any age.

You taught me how to survive the hardships of disappointment and grief. You lost a baby when you were young, you felt it wither in your womb, and yet you found me, in that smoldering cabin, and suckled me, and nurtured me as you would have nurtured the baby you lost. When I lost Benjamin, and was still swollen, and my eyes poured tears those weeks and months, you nurtured me again, brought me back to life, and to hope. I lost dear Lawrence, too, and again your spirit—you have ever been spirited—showed me how to live. It still does.

Do you remember when I was a schoolgirl, afraid to make the speech I had written as my class representative? I had memorized it, and spoken it under my breath night after night. But I could not give it voice. "Under your bed," you commanded me. "Now say your speech to the boards above, to the ticking in your mattress." I mumbled the speech.

"I didn't hear you, Nell," you said, and demanded I speak it again, louder. I trained my eye on a knot in a wooden slat. I pretended it was a tunnel, and I shouted my words down that tunnel so that they might be heard forever. I told you what I did.

"That knot is not a tunnel, it is an eye. It is my eye. Look at me, and make your words disappear into me this time." I did, all the time pretending your eye was a knot of wood. I did the same thing when I delivered the speech to my classroom, full of students and parents. I remember parts of it still, the parts, I dare say, that you helped me think through. "We have climbed onto but one branch of the tree that is knowledge. Higher branches dare us to climb higher. Each branch has many leaves, each leaf something new to learn." Oh, Mother Jo, you are still in the tree, as am I, climbing. Thank you for teaching me, for learning with me, for nurturing me throughout my life.

I was once asked by my minister why I was so compelled to turn everything into a "cause." I think he was being polite, wondering why so much of my life was spent battling with the world—over slavery, over science, evolution, fossils, and the age of the earth. I wonder if I was just lucky enough to live in a time of causes, and that I allowed the world to shape me, or whether I was so shaped as to make my time on earth a time of great causes? Perhaps, Mother Jo, a little of each? I recognize the "you" that is part of "me"—shaped and shaper, sculpted and sculptor, branched and brancher. You taught me that the more you know about the past, the more you can be present. I thank you for your wisdom in that, but even more for your example, which has ever guided me through both hardship and ease, through difficulty and through stars, as we say here in Kansas. Ad astra per aspera. That might have been your motto, as well.

I hope to be able to visit you soon. I will come as soon as it is temperate enough to travel. On the way home, I will stop at the home of Sally Miller. Her husband died just after Thanksgiving of last year, and she will be convinced to join me in Kansas.

Your loving daughter,
Nell

Diary Entry

The mind, asleep, is ever busy, and in a moment of near wakefulness I stood, my dress unbuttoned from the top, beside a bluff overlooking a vast river. My breasts were swollen, as they were both times I was with child. They were tender to the touch, and I bent in pain. Milk leaked onto rock, liquid staining stone, then the dark dribbles turned white and hardened into fossil. When I reached to feel the new formations they disappeared and I awoke sobbing.

My mother told me the story of losing her first baby, of the swollen tenderness at her breast that lasted for weeks as her body adjusted itself to loss. But she had no mother to console her, only her brothers and her pa, and they were outlaws and not given to tenderness. She continued the pregnancy by wrapping herself each day, swaddling her withering belly rather than a child, so that they might not beat her. Then she escaped them. When she found me in the smoldering ruins of our Onnen cabin, her heart, she said, leaped. Her breasts tingled. She knew she could feed me. Others thought her deranged, far as she was from her pregnancy, but she persisted and her milk let down, as did her tears.

When I lost my babies I thought of Mother Jo, her body not quite returned to itself. "Fate," she said, "brought us together. I was not your mother, but I could mother you. We saved each other's lives!"

My life has been saved. Is there any difference between tears, milk, stone?

Letter from Sister Mary

Saturday, July 5, 1890
Pine Bluff, AR

My dearest Nell—

I write to break the news of the death of our mother, Jo. We saw her last on her eightieth birthday, some weeks ago. Yes, she received your package with the stone and letter inside. She admired the rock and your successes in the science of fossils, and, as always, she cherished your letter, which she put with so many others you have sent dutifully over the years. I enclose them, as they most rightfully belong to you. And I return the fossil rock you sent her, along with another.

You may remember the stone that sat on the mantel these many years, large as an ostrich egg. I never asked Mother about it, though she dusted it dutifully these many years. On her birthday, perhaps sensing her impending death, she asked that you have it. "Write to her, if I haven't," she instructed me. "Please tell her that the rock came from near the Hatchie River, from the burned home of her first parents, that I picked it up and thrust it into my saddlebag. We never broke it open, though Robert wanted to." Nell, I don't know that she wrote those words to you, for she was frail even then.

We arrived the same day the Jacksons sent a rider to us, and found the cabin tidy and clean. We saw no signs of pain or struggle, so we hope, as I'm sure you do, that she died peacefully and with a heart full of the world to come. She is buried beside Robert, and we will see to the stone. On your next visit we will take you to Pioneer Cemetery. Charles and Henry and Francis all hope to see you, for though you have met your nephew's wives, you have yet to meet their children, and yet to coo over Francis's beau. You have yet to meet my great-grandchild, little Abigail—who would think I would be blessed with one already?

Nell, I miss you. Mother's death has brought so many memories of our lives together before you went to Kansas with Solomon Doerr. I know you have a fine life. But don't forget your humble beginnings and those who have loved you so truly these many, many years. Write if you feel you need anything from Mother's house. We will leave it as is for the time being, as it is close at hand, and a useful property as well. It is your inheritance, as well, so let your wishes be known.

Sent with love and shared sympathy.

Your sister,
Mary

P.S. I am also enclosing the letters you have sent to me these many years, as no doubt you will someday want them with your diaries and other publications—I feel you will be an important person, one who will be studied. I am less likely to be the object of anyone's curiosity.

Diary Entry

The stone is a geode, and it rested on the mantel so long we did not even notice it. That it was gathered from the place of my birth and near death is a shock to me. How much else was kept from me of my circumstances before Robert and Jo Johnson rescued me from a smoldering cabin and claimed me as their own? Who were my parents? Shall I always be doomed to live many lives, to be many persons? Baby Onnen became Nell Johnson. Nell Johnson became Mrs. Solomon Doerr. Mrs. Solomon Doerr became Widow Doerr. Widow Doerr became the shunned fossil hunter and scandal. The shunned fossil hunter and scandal became the respected supplier of the National Museum. The respected supplier became a writer whose words were presented to the National Academy. And now she becomes a motherless child, sent a rock for heritage.

I broke the rock, one clean hit of hammer on chisel. Each half was a cave full of purple crystals, amethyst, like sharp teeth, jagged, mirroring light, color softening at the points, a beauty hidden all these years. My father knew what was inside. He wanted to break the rock. But he did not. As I have learned from my own studies, much of what we know is on the surface only. Many think we are not meant to delve deeply. We are afraid to break the rock. Who knows what we might find inside? I have broken the rock and found beauty. Over and over I have broken the rock.

AFTERWORD

In writing *Found Documents from the Life of Nell Johnson Doerr*, I had the pleasure of fabricating the history of a woman whose life spanned the years 1825 to approximately 1890. Although Nell Doerr did not exist, I tried to be accurate with place and historical events. All documents, drawings, letters, notes, and diary entries are completely invented, though I tried to be true to the styles and sensibilities of those times. I have always enjoyed using what I call "false documents" within my fiction: recipes, menus, notes, postcards, letters, poems, and newspaper articles. Recently, this kind of writing has been labelled "archival fiction," and that fits *Found*, with its being comprised entirely of a found archive.

Nell Johnson Doerr was also found. She made her first appearance in my novel *rode*, as an infant discovered in the smoldering cabin of her parents and adopted by Robert and Jo Johnson as they made their way to Arkansas territory to live in the Pine Bluff area. There, they became involved in the Underground Railroad. Nell's story is one of slavery and freedom, of loss and discovery, of a time when much of science was practiced by amateur collectors interested in new theories and classifications of the known world. The sciences of the nineteenth century owe much to people like Nell Johnson Doerr, driven by curiosity to free themselves from the bonds of conventional thought and practice. Her beliefs—in freedom, democracy, education, and knowledge—make her representative of the Kansas of her times, a Kansas that was at the center of what was important to the nation: abolition, women's rights, temperance, free thought, public education, and public health and welfare.

ACKNOWLEDGMENTS

Jeffrey Ann Goudie has always been my greatest support, my most critical editor, and my most astute reader. I am lucky that she is also my wife, and the love of my life. My daughter, Eleanor Goudie-Averill, read *Found* in various iterations, and her enthusiasm and thoughtful insights buoyed me in the process of writing. I thank my son, Alexander Goudie-Averill, for waiting so tolerantly when his mother and father stooped to find fossils, including bryozoans, on mountain trails in New Mexico. The same fossils found in northeast Kansas are also prevalent in the Sangre de Cristos at 8,500 feet. My family has had the good fortune of spending time at the Pecos Wilderness cabin my late father-in-law, Jim Goudie, a geologist, bought over forty years ago. Thanks to Ruth Goudie for sustaining the property, and thus giving us the chance to find fossils there.

Fossils have always been an interest of mine, but research helped me understand them fully enough to create a character who could find and study them. I particularly thank the University of Kansas Spencer Research Library (Archivist Rebecca Schulte and staff), Kansas State University Archives (Archivist Cliff Hight and staff), Katie Armitage and Monica Davis of the Watkins Community Museum, and the University of Kansas Invertebrate Collection and staff. Geoglogists Will Gilliland (Washburn University), Roy Beckemeyer (longtime coeditor of the *Transactions of the Kansas Academy of Sciences*), and Rex Buchanan (Kansas Geological Survey) loaned me material. Roy and Rex were kind enough to read *Found* in manuscript form with an eye not only to accuracy about fossils, but accuracy about when scientists knew what they knew about the fossil record. Historical accuracy was also paramount, and I thank Virgil Dean, longtime editor of *Kansas History: A Journal of the Central Plains*, for his knowledge of Lawrence, and Kansas, and Kansans, and for reading *Found* for its history. Given so much help, I can only hope for authenticity in my science and history. Any errors are exclusively my own.

Research takes time and resources, and Washburn University, where I served from 1980 to 2017 as writer-in-residence and professor of English, has been generous with both. I had a sabbatical for the final writing of *Found*, and small research grants to support research and illustrations. The Washburn University Center for Kansas Studies supported travel for research as well. One of those trips took me to Western Kansas, where I stayed with Myrna and Elmer Schlegel along the Saline River, among fossil-rich chalk bluffs, and toured the Sternberg Museum at Fort Hays State University with paleontologist Mike Everhart, who has dug fossils of mosasaurs on the Schlegel place.

Writing, except in its earliest stages, is highly collaborative for me. The longstanding Topeka Men's Group listens to, discusses, and supports my efforts at our yearly camp-outs. My colleagues at the university first learned about, and critiqued, early sections of *Found* in a Washburn University College of Arts and Science interdisciplinary faculty colloquium titled WALK. My writer friends do great service in their willingness to read, edit, and comment on early drafts. Thanks particularly to Catherine Browder Morris, Karen Barron, and Steve Sherwood for improving the novel. Finally, my deep appreciation to artist Clint Ricketts for help with the Figures in *Found*; we have collaborated before, on a Garden Plots website, and the collaboration always teaches me more about my work, and Clint's.

Other writers inspire me. Thanks to Charles Darwin (*On the Origin of Species*), Oliver Sacks (*On the Move*), Tracey Chevalier (*Remarkable Creatures*), and Elizabeth Gilbert (*The Signature of All Things*) for the brilliance of their work and their perspectives on science.

Finally, books are not just written—they have to be submitted, read, accepted, copyedited, designed, put between covers, promoted, and sold. Thanks to editor Elise McHugh and the University of New Mexico Press for doing such fine work. On the home front, Nikki Daniels of the Washburn University Bookstore (The Ichabod Shop) helps with promotion and local sales of my novels.

My apologies to any and all I should have thanked. If I haven't remembered you, please know that I haven't forgotten you.